Darkness
in the
City of
Light

Darkness in the City of Light

Tony Curtis

Seren is the book imprint of
Poetry Wales Press Ltd,
4 Derwen Road, Bridgend, Wales, CF31 1LH

www.serenbooks.com
facebook.com/SerenBooks
Twitter: @SerenBooks

This is a work of fiction.

ISBN: 9781781726136
Ebook: 9781781726402

A CIP record for this title is available from the British Library.

The publisher acknowledges the financial assistance
of the Books Council of Wales.

Cover Photograph: Adolf Hitler, German Nazi dictator,
inspecting occupied Paris, France, 1940. Artist: Unknown
The Print Collector / Alamy Stock Photo

Printed by Pulsio Print.

Darkness
in the
City of
Light

Never trust the teller, trust the tale – D.H. Lawrence

1
In the City of Light

June, 1945 Police headquarters, Paris

A woman's heels approach down a long corridor
stopping outside a room marked 'The Petiot Case'.
She unlocks the door and switches on two stark, swinging bulbs.
She is dressed in a suit,
her make-up is exact, her hair in fashion.
She sees a chaos of suitcases, clothes,
personal effects –

She reads and checks the list on her clipboard:

43 bodices/
2 pairs of sock suspenders/
4 cardigans/
6 men's hats/
13 sanitary pads/
35 belts/
18 undervests/
29 brassières/
60 pairs of underpants/
6 pairs of slacks/
5 fur coats/
13 negligées/
11 hatpins/
48 scarves/
77 pairs of gloves (some missing)/
26 women's handkerchiefs/
79 dresses/
31 combinations/
14 men's raincoats/
115 men's shirts/
28 suits/
66 pairs of shoes (several missing)/

104 detachable collars/
94 cufflinks (some gold)/
13 nightshirts/
9 sheets/
13 pillowcases/
63 towels/
9 table clothes/
7 cultured-pearl necklaces/
5 manicure files
12 pairs of spectacles/
13 tram tickets unused/

Items taken from rue Caumartin and rue la Sueur – All checked, though three wallets and six purses are unaccounted for...

1940, June 28th, Arno Breker's Paris

We were driven in the black Mercedes sedan, quite discreetly, with just two other cars, down an empty Champs Elysée on a glorious day. 6.a.m. The sun was rising on our celebrations. I sat next to Albert Speer just behind the Führer, who was quite quiet, as if soaking in the significance of the moment. He must have dreamt of this victory through the months of trench mud and the carnage of the Flanders campaign. Paris was a distant goal that proved to be beyond us. The scything plan to circle down through Belgium had not been completed. That time. Our fighting men had been let down by politics and the Jews. But the French have proved stupid again and clearly have learned nothing. There were no trenches this time. Our armour and columns swept through Belgium. It is all ours.

'This is a jewel, indeed. But you two men will build Berlin into a colossus which will cast this place into the shadows. And now we will walk before the Eiffel Tower and show the world what we have done.' The Führer is more determined than triumphant. 'I decline to march in triumph at the head of my troops here,' he said, 'we shall secure an *entente franco-allemande* when these people come to their senses and accept our victory and the new world order.'

Our first stop was the Opera, that neo-baroque masterpiece by Garnier. That was the Fuhrer's choice, his favourite building, he said.

Down the Champs Élyseés to the Trocadero and the tomb of The Unknown Soldier. One of those dug out of the mud across the killing fields from our leader and his platoon. Fate determined such different ends. Hitler instructed his photographer, Heinrich Hoffman, "Take me in front of this view of the Eiffel Tower; then the next one at Buckingham Palace and then the skyscrapers."

At Les Invalides, Adolf Hitler stood quietly before the tomb of Napoleon; he will more than emulate the conqueror and surely avoid the mistakes which led to that great man's downfall. Then to the Parthenon.

At Montparnasse we were kept away from the small groups of visitors and looked across the so-called city of light.

Three days before, in the forest of Compiègne, such theatre: he ordered that they bring the railway carriage to the position in the village of Pethondes where the French and the British had humiliated us in 1918. As the French signed their surrender, the Fuhrer rose, turned his back on them and walked out.

This morning we took the short flight from Compiègne to Le Bourget airport. The land, our land, was dark and rose-hued. Speer was impressed by the sight of Paris stretched out before us. He will surely rise to the task of exceeding whatever they have done here. 'Berlin will be the centre of Europe, the world's great capital, envied by all.' Hitler has ordered him to measure the Champ-Élysées and ensure that our Unter den Linden in Berlin is twenty metres wider.

'And Breker's statues will line the grand avenues and parks,' he says. I assure the Führer that my studio is already a substantial workshop and my assistants are up to the task, no matter how ambitious.

The matter of a victory parade has been raised during our visit. Colonel Speidel, our city commander is in favour, but it will not happen. The Fuhrer said, "I am not in the mood for a victory parade. We are not at the end of this thing yet. I have long considered whether we should destroy this city. But it will not be necessary. When we have realised our dreams of Berlin, this place will be no more than a shadow by comparison."

Our progress through the city was like a private tour of an open-air museum. Paris was an empty shell, so many have fled south and into the country. At times in our car the Führer was strangely quiet – subdued even, between awe and contemplation. By nine o'clock we were back at Le Bourget to fly out. In victory the Führer had spent a bare three hours in the city of his greatest conquest.

Though there is a steely determined vision to Adolf Hitler. He will prevail and we Germans with him.

Heil Hitler.

Orders of Occupation for all Soldiers, June 31st, 1940.

- Every soldier shall at all times exhibit the sharpest discipline, exemplary conduct and diligence in the duties of occupation and security.
- When on patrol or off duty on the street there should be no smoking or loosening of jackets and ties.
- Army personnel are forbidden from entering public places of entertainment, cinemas and clubs: there will be established our own Soldatenkinos for the exclusive use of German personnel.
- All French road crossings and general traffic regulations should be adhered to unless German security issues are compromised by such compliance.
- Swimming in the river Seine is strictly forbidden.
- Singing and dancing in public is strictly forbidden.
- There shall be no association with black or Jewish women.
- Personal shopping should be conducted solely through our military department stores and liquor outlets. Souvenirs may be purchased at the military boutiques in the Bois de Boulogne area.
- Personnel are encouraged to spend their free time in the Soldatenheim for reasons of safety and security.
- Abteil Für Deutsche carriages are reserved for personnel when travel on the Metro is unavoidable.
- The frequenting of brothels and other establishments on the published forbidden list will be dealt with as matters of the most serious discipline.
- From henceforth, the official time in the city of Paris will be that of Berlin time.

TIPS FOR THE "OCCUPIED"

- *Street sellers, you may offer the Boches maps of Paris and phrasebooks; they spill out of buses, pour out in front of Notre-Dame and the Panthéon; every one of them has a camera to his eye. Be under no illusion: they are not tourists.*
- *They are the victors. Act correctly with them, as we must. But don't go out of your way.*
- *If one of them speaks to you in German, make a sign of "Je ne comprend pas". Excuse yourself and move on.*
- *If they ask for a light, offer your cigarette. Never, not for a long time, have we refused a light to anyone—not even to our enemy.*
- *If they think it useful to seduce us, to lower our guard, by offering concerts in public places, you do not have to attend, have other appointments. Stay at home, or go to the countryside to listen to the bird song of France.*
- *Reading our newspapers has never been good if one wanted to learn good habits of our language. Now, the Parisian daily newspapers no longer even think in decent French.*
- *Act with sang froid, keep cool and calm; but feed your anger within your breast. It will prove useful when the time comes.*
- *It is such an imposition to be made to return home at 11 p.m. But we know that this means you can listen to English radio and learn the truth.*

The Beginning of an Infection

They look just like us, or like the best of our men when they marched north to the war, but these Germans seem taller, more upright, with the straight backs of those who know they have won through. Some of them, taking off their helmets, are young and they look around them wide-eyed like schoolboys on a culture trip: 'Where is the Eiffel Tower? Is that the famous cathedral? May one swim safely in the river?'

Mothers who had called their children back in to the apartment blocks are venturing out again. Kids gaze up in amazement at the huge trucks and armoured cars. The soldiers start to throw down chocolate bars – and who can stop the children reaching for them? As they unwrap these sweets we see that they are French chocolates: they are gifting us their lootings. Soon there will be lots of little Fritzes for them to play with…

In the following days more and more young women are drawn to these men; some of whom have enough of our language to compliment and flirt. They are like bitches in heat. And so it begins: we are conquered and will accommodate the Germans. They will argue that it is in both our interests to come to an understanding. It is only in the weeks that follow that we realise that we are to live on rations of their choosing and that the produce of our fields will go to the feeding of their army, their war of expansion.

They seem to know the city as well as we do – where are the rich Jews' houses in the 8th and the 16th? Which of our government offices will best suit their plans to rule Paris? How does the Metro function?

Within weeks the road signs are in German. Our traffic gendarmes are controlling the traffic with the necessary priorities. The radio, the Metro, the restaurants and hotels are no longer ours. The Feldmans who occupy the floor below ours are now wearing the Star of David which they had to sew on to their own coats.

My sister Madeleine, who works as a nurse in the American Hospital, came home this evening in tears: the surgeon and hospital director Professor Martel has killed himself. He let it be known that he could not live with a German infection in his city.

November 11th, 1940

My fellow students and patriots – I urge you all to go to no classes this day but to assemble on our national holiday and commemorate the Victory that will surely be ours again, despite the heel of the invaders.

We shall march in an orderly fashion down the Avenue des Champs-Élysées to the Arc de Triomphe and honour the Unknown Soldier of France. This is our right and our duty! We shall sing the Marseillaise in defiance of the occupier. We shall link arms and show our solidarity as Frenchmen, which cannot be broken.

Pass on this leaflet and tell your fellows to support the cause.

Notice of the Execution of a man in connection with public order requirements.

The engineer Jacques Bonsergent was shot this morning. He had received a death sentence from the German Military tribunal following his conviction of an offence of violence towards a member of the German army committed on November 11th.

Paris, 23rd December 1940
The Military Command of France

The First Christmas

They call that justice. I knew Bonsergent, a good man, railway worker, no trouble. A fine young man. Seems he and some mates were coming back from a friend's wedding out in one of the villages. A little tipsy – why not? Just around the corner from Gare Saint-Lazare these men run into a gang of bottled-up Germans and the bastards have a go at them. What – are they going to kiss the Boches and wave them by? Couple of shoulders nudged, hardly a punch thrown, words shouted.

But the Boches collar Jacques and drag him to the barracks. For a good kicking, no doubt – that's what you expect from those pricks. But this execution weeks later? Pour encourager…

Some fucking Christmas present.

These evil bastards are losing it. They have forgotten where they are. We will remember this and make them remember this and pay for it.

The XXIInd Biennale

This endless summer – Brussels, Paris – and in Venice
Our white-sailed yacht with the men working aloft
Taking its place with a flotilla on the milky green waters
Of the lagoon between the Lido and St Mark's.

Last night Joseph was in triumph on the balcony of the palace
With minister Alfieri echoing his praise of il Duce;
The crowd packed into the torch-lit square,
Then jostling to get closer to us at the Café Florian.

This Biennale celebrates Veronese, such flesh, what light,
But Sciltian's modern tricks – his trompe l'oeil and nature morte,
Impressed us too. Of course, there are no British or French this
        year,
And the Americans are degenerate, impure; they have no art.

Here on the lagoon one can put aside the concerns of war:
Paris is ours and London will follow. Joseph is relaxed
in his white slacks, hat and sunglasses; I still wear Chanel.
Though each day the aeroplane brings state papers to be read.

One dark cloud: his staff, hearing him say how much he missed
His Airedale, flew over today with the dog on board – fools!
The Reich Minister was furious at the upset caused;
We've left the poor thing to be cared for at the Hotel Danieli.

By such concern great men show themselves human.
This summer's memories we shall treasure: the art pavilions,
The evenings' hot chocolate, our jewels and furs, the joyous,
        plaintive violins.
And St Mark's campanile lit at its peak like some great candle or
        chimney.

A Consultation at rue Caumartin

Here is a comfortable chair. Let me light your cigarette. I am Doctor Marcel Petiot. It is best that you are relaxed and know that you are in safe hands. I have welcomed others who have come from our mutual friend Monsieur Estébéteguy, A man who has made a success of things.

Mademoiselle Gisèle, let me make it clear that I do not judge, that is for others. If I, a medical practitioner and true Frenchman, may be able to help in such a delicate matter, then so be it.

No, no, let us not talk about money at such a time. And you have acted wisely in coming to Dr Petiot's office rather than those dark alleys and dubious women who say that they can perform such things.

So, I do not care to know about the father – German or one of ours – a woman has to survive as best she can in these awful times.

Apologies, my hands will be cold – who can heat an apartment now? Even a doctor cannot get the coal he needs. But, and this is more important, I do have sources for all the medicines and drugs required in my practice, Adrien Estébéteguy and his contacts ensure that. You shall want for nothing before, during and after the procedure.

Who would wish to bring an innocent child into this mess? The Church and the Vichy would have all you women doing that. Breeding like cats. For France.

Now, if you would like to come over to this side of the room into the light…

Ah, yes, yes, I think perhaps we might meet again at my rue le Sueur rooms. For the injections, you understand. You may wish for Adrien le Basque to accompany you. Then matters may be settled.

From an Officer's Diaries – 1

I walked back from the office to lunch with Michelle, cutting through le Parc Monceau. It is so cold, ice on the pond. A nanny pushing her pram past me seemed to quicken her pace; she slid a look across to me and I felt it to be between annoyance and intrigue. Did she mutter, "Boche"? What strange creatures we must seem to the ordinary French. Yet are we not all God's own?

*

My dealer in the unassuming little place on the left bank has promised a Goya etching and is talking of a small Poussin drawing on its way. A temptation not to be resisted. Under the Occupation many gems and treasures, little and great are becoming available. The Bureau grabs most of the really good things for shipping back to Berlin to Goering, whose collection must now be rivalling that of the Louvre – Monets, Renoirs, even Pissarro whose Jewish heritage can be quietly forgotten when Nature's beauty is celebrated. He has a particular liking for Cranachs. At the Jeu de Paume he plundered like a schoolgirl given the freedom of a department store.

*

I have a locked filing cabinet for the sensitive intelligence reports. This morning I slide out one drawer for the reports of the shooting on the hostages taken at Nantes in reprisal for the murder of one of our naval cadets. Of course, there was nothing of importance in their final statements and letters. How could there be, they were picked at random from that community. It is the very arbitrariness wherein lies the power to subdue and coerce. However, I shall endeavour to preserve their words – "courage", "remember", "mother" and "farewell" are the most frequent. There is honesty in the very lack of originality of the writing. One man wants his family to remember to feed their hidden pig, which is to be killed on the eve of La Toussaint.

*

Yesterday we visited P in his apartment on the Quai Voltaire. He keeps rooms there with a fine view over the roofs of Saint-Germain-des-Prés. He has a maid who feeds the fires and cooks breakfast. Here, without his uniform, he becomes more natural and is good company. Books everywhere, some fine.

A signed Proust on the coffee table. Last week, he said, Cocteau visited and read some dialogue from his new play. I think there is a type of writer who projects his dreams and confusions out on to the stage so that he may recognise them, regardless of what sense they may have for the audience.

*

Lunch at Au Caneton with Lucy. One has to order crêpes and the caviar which one spreads between the little pancakes. These were my weekly treat when I visited in the `thirties. Some things are not meant to change and are the actions and habits that keep us afloat. We are all on the same voyage.

*

One of my Left Bank dealers has a dark and close store with the treasures I prize: today, a 1623 Histoire Générale des Larrons by d'Aubricourt, with a fine leather binding, almost no scuff marks. Also, a first edition of A High Wind in Jamaica, by Richard Hughes, in the American first by Harper & Sons under its title The Innocent Voyage – full red goat skin, very rare and an exceptional find here on the banks of the Seine. A voyage on which innocence is lost and an entry into adulthood by virtue of threats and violence. Truly, a book for our times.

*

Three mornings stuck in the Hôtel Lutétia this week. Checking files and looking for references to a "Henri" who had gone missing and of whom J was anxious to hear. Nothing. But at least I was on a different floor from the places where my colleagues in the Abwehr conduct their affairs of interrogatoire forcée. This is not a battlefield; there are seldom defined lines of strategy. No rules of engagement.

*

At Maxim's for lunch with friends I shared my prized copy of the Hughes, of which they knew little. On my return walk down Rue Royale I passed two young girls wearing the yellow star, which they have to pay for out of their clothes ration coupons. Then several others, men and women: never had I felt so conspicuous in my army uniform.

*

A fine evening at General H's. Lots of top brass and a sprinkling of the best of the French – H has always been a cultured man whose nose has wrinkled at many of the little house painter's rantings and obsessions. Picasso, some of whose work we burned at the Jeu de Paume along with other degenerates Miró and Ernst a few months back. He is a small but twinkling man. An aura about him which some men and, apparently, most women are drawn to. Count Keyserling in the most comfortable chair; distant, dreaming as much as watching the movement of the room. Old money, old land, bestows a natural superiority that does not even know it is no longer of our world. How did these people think that they could control the ranting corporal and the mob that have taken over?

LES LETTRES
françaises

June 1942

WE MUST BE WITNESSES TO THE TRUTH!

I can report that I saw a train pass by, going north out of the city – in the first car there were uniformed men, our French police and German soldiers.

Then, cattle trucks which had been sealed tight by solder and the doors secured by chains. Small arms, children's arms stretched through the barred windows. Their little hands fluttered like trapped birds on a market stall.

As the train slowed down at the junction, I could hear their calls, "Maman!" over the grinding of the axles and the clanging of the couplings. So, we too must shout out above that clamour of metal and coldness. We must protest the yellow star, the abductions of women and children, the shootings of fathers.

There is only one way, Comrades – we must bear witness to the persecution of a whole people. They may look like us and speak our language, they may not look like us and not speak our language, but we owe it to them to witness their fate. We owe it to our readers and fellow citizens to write and speak of this as long as it shall continue.

WE MUST BEAR WITNESS!

Schutzstaffel Reichsführer Heinrich Himmler
Memo: strategies for dealing with attacks on our forces in France
January 13th 1943.

The shooting or other means of execution of hostages taken in retaliation for the attacks on Germans is to be replaced whenever possible by the deportation for forced labour and other actions. Many may be simply dealt with through military courts and become lost in that process. This will ensure that opposition to our enforcement of the law will be less concentrated and easier to deal with. We cannot waste resources of time and men on such matters.

Where execution does take place there will be clear orders and procedures:

Hanging should be carried out by fellow prisoners. They will be offered payment in the form of cigarettes – five for each criminal hanged should be appropriate.

Corpses should be disposed of in the crematorium or, where possible, utilized by the anatomy classes of nearby universities. If neither action is possible, then these bodies should be buried in Jewish cemeteries or in those sections of municipal cemeteries allocated for suicides.

Communists, bandits – those guilty of direct action against our troops should face the firing squad. These should consist of at least six soldiers with rifles. They should take their position five paces from the condemned man. This work is not to be regarded as special duty. It is what every soldier has been trained to do without question.

Paris, July 1943

I.

Sleep, durme, durme, little one,
Listen to your mother's song.
Sleep, sleep to the words I sing,
This world can do you no more wrong.

Durme, durme, sleep my precious son.
The song my mother sang to me
Will take you safe to Israel's shore
Through green meadows, the warm sea.

This room is cold, damp, and I have the pattering
of mice in the walls for company.
While little Reuben turns in his sleep,
his lips dry and moving in dreams.

Three knocks for Isaac –do not open the door for anyone else.

'Isaac! I was so worried – but you've got bread.'

'Bread, but no meat, there's little to be had, but a sausage
and these two apples.'

'With my wedding ring you couldn't get more?
And what did Joseph say? Has he got the papers?
Is Rachel safe? And Ruth?'

'Joseph didn't come.'

'What? He promised. The papers –
what about the papers for us?'

'There are no papers. And there's something else –
they are rounding up Jews throughout the city.
Here in Paris.'

"It's probably a census, checking people, do you think?"

'They are herding them like sheep, round-ups.
In the 15th and 16th last week, now everywhere.'

'I told you it was best to stay here, as long as we say
we are Dutch. Monsieur Baudet believes we are Dutch.
And as long as we pay, he will not ask too much.
We can lie low, can't we? Lie low
and just go out to barter for what we need.
For what Reuben needs.'

'They are taking the children too.
All the children over three years are being taken.
They have special schools, they say.'

'They are taking our children? Why?
They want to take them to their schools and turn them in to
        Nazis?'

'They are doing it – children pulled screaming from their
        parents
and the men and women driven away in army trucks
to Parc de Princes and the Velodrome d'Hiver –
they are no longer racing bikes and ice skating there.
The adults are going in trains to labour camps in the East,
who knows – Germany, Poland?

There is a story of a woman who killed her five children and
        herself.'
'This is mad. We must fight them. We have to be crafty.
Five children – that's lies. Do you believe that?'

'All the Jews have been taken from the Rothschild Hospital,
Some of them after operations – all piled into trucks.
Are the Germans in such a state that they need cripples in their
camps?'

'They need beds for their soldiers, perhaps, billets…'

'In Paris? It's not for billets. They are killing us.
I tell you, they are killing all of us.
They have made up their minds and they will do it.
They have the power, they can do what they like,
so they will kill all the Jews.'

'God help us!'

'We must go, sell everything we have All the stuff in your case.
There may be a way out, for money.'

'We have no choice, now.'

'The tunnels cost money, but I have the name of a contact,
a café in the Sixteenth… A contact, a proven contact.
He's a doctor, reliable. Doctor Petiot.
If I give him the ruby ring, your grandmother Ruth's,
he will find a way for us. That second ring will do it, they say,
it is a fine odem, dark pigeon's blood.'

'Rubies are the healing stone. They are good luck'.

'What need have we for jewelry, wherever we are going?'

II.

Here, Monsieur, let me whisper to you – The Fly-Tox Method…

Meet Fourrier at the barbershop. You must have ready the
    identity papers,
60,000 francs, and ten photographs for false papers.
Two suitcases only.
You must pack only what you really want to keep,
things which are precious.
Photographs of loved ones are risky.
These are dangerous times. Tell no-one.
Dr Eugène – an eminent man, I assure you –
an assumed name, you understand – will administer
an injection. It is not unpleasant to be put to sleep
and it is, believe me, essential to his method.
It is hard, I know, but soon you will wake to find
all your worries are over. Trust us:
this is business, but also love of our fellow man.

III.

Hotel Central
Buenos Aires
12th of November 1943

Ma Cherie,

       I am safe here. Thanks to Dr Eugène.
and his organisation.
Do not worry.
When the time comes do everything he tells you.
Bring the rest of the money, but most of all yourself.

I miss you so much. I miss Paris.
Soon these dark times will be
a distant memory,
no more than smoke to be blown away.
Until the day
we kiss again,

Your loving,
　　　Simon

It is good to finally get a letter. But he doesn't mention Emile: a father does not write of his son?

Fourrier's on rue des Mathurins

The Doctor has been a regular, for years,
shave, a trim. A gent who paid and held a good conversation,
helped me too with a spot of bother with my stomach.
I've known him for a good time, before the Occupation,

he's just a couple of streets away.
What he says is his word: you can trust Petiot
with your life – I swear.
He'll get you out and no questions asked.

Do as he says: bring your best clothes, jewels,
whatever you hold precious and wish to keep.
Three days, three days to process things –
your ten photographs, the new papers.

Trust me, trust the barber: take no chance.
What price a life? Twenty-five thousand francs.

I swear I gave him the idea, it was mine.
Told him about those cyclists who broke away from their race
and headed straight over into Vichy.
Simple. No-one could catch them.

He said he kept a packed suitcase by his front door,
always ready for the off. Be prepared in shitty times.
he gives fair service to one and all,
Jews, communists, people leaving behind crimes.

Draw a shining sun on the back of a cent francs note,
circle the "Cent Francs" to touch Liberty's nose

and the locks of the putti. Tear in half.
When you are safely away, send one half back as proof.

Trust me, trust the barber: take no chance.
I've had my razor on the neck of la belle France.

My life so far

This will be my last entry. We have been waiting for the door-bell to ring and now it has, loud and hard and prolonged. They have taken father. It seemed that our family would be safe, as French professionals, working for generations in the law and science and education in Paris. But now I must accept that we are no different to the others – the Hungarians, the Poles, the Czechs, those who came to this city to be safe from the persecution in their own countries. They are being rounded up in the Marais and the 20th. It is our own police force who are responsible for this. People are taken to police stations and then, it is said, to Drancy in the north of the city.

At first, I wore my star with a sort of pride. Some would look away, but many smiled and put their thumbs up or came and spoke – the weather, the rationing, the uncertain Métro. Yesterday a young couple waiting at the entrance to the Place de l'Étoile turned to smile at me and said, 'It's disgusting, what they are doing to you. Don't worry, they will have to wear their swastika with shame for the rest of their lives.'

The hardest thing to bear is the sight of small children having to wear the star: it as if they have been branded. How would I have felt a few years ago as a young girl having to wear such a thing?

This year I am not allowed to register at the Sorbonne. I still go to the lectures and follow up on the reading, though I have to be home by six every evening. Some students have turned away from me, but others are happy to talk to me and debate points of imagery as if nothing had changed. I am falling "half in love" with Keats. Also, a boy I keep seeing in the library in the foreign literatures stacks.

Marie said that she had heard of an incident in the Metro when a German officer had objected to a woman with the star sitting in the first-class carriage and pulled the red cord. When she moved to the designated last carriage, so did all the other passengers, leaving the German absurdly on his own with no-one left to bully.

We have always lived on the Left Bank and, in a sense, the events the other side of river have always seemed part of another world. We have the Champs de Mars and the Latin Quarter. Walking down Boulevard Saint-Michel in the spring crowds it is as if nothing had really changed. From Rue Soufflot to Boulevard Saint-Germain I feel free, as always, a natural citizen of Paris. Perhaps we will come through this present madness and the cafés, the Seine, the Sorbonne and the Louvre will be here as always and the city will be reclaimed by us again. I have not yet planned out my life, so perhaps that is a good thing.

(I shall leave this journal in the hands of our cook, Monique, for safe keeping. I trust that she will have it intact – perhaps with a few flour and butter stains – for me to continue when we return.)

A birthday night out
Saturday August 15th, 1943

Marcel was especially kind and considerate. For my birthday he took me to the One Two Two Club where Edith Piaf was singing – a table "reserved for Petiot". The little robin was in good voice and I enjoyed it greatly. She is such a small woman, but seemed to grow bigger under the lights and once she had sung two or three songs. I wore the ruby ring Marcel had bought for me, it glinted like a drop of blood on my finger.

There were a lot of Boches officers in the audience, but they were more interested in the dancing girls. And buying champagne for their noisy parties. There were also lots of feathered girls with little on. I think that this club may also be a brothel.

For much of the evening Marcel was engaged in deep conversations with a thick-set man who he called "Le Basque". I tried to make friends with his woman, Gisèle, but she seemed quite cold and distant. And dull. Little more than a girl, really.

Marcel later apologized for neglecting me, but I did enjoy the singing and the dancing routines. And, anyway, he said he had important business dealings with this Adrien le Basque, who was able to supply the drugs needed for Marcel's practice and which are so difficult to obtain at these times. I did not take to this man. He seemed not quite the type for us to have dealings with. Still, these are awkward days and the city must make peace with all sorts of people and all manners of things if we are to get through. To survive such times is good, but to prosper is remarkable. Marcel is a remarkable man. I am fortunate.

On the ride home I couldn't get out of my head the chorus that the little robin had sung:

My man plays his accordion
like a dream
It keeps my heart beating strong.
In Paris my lover and my song
Take me through the darkest storm.

Silly songs and words. They keep us going.

Drancy Internment Camp, north Paris, 1943.

Here we can see and talk to our families through the wire from time to time. Shouting from block to block, voices bouncing off the bare concrete walls. Food and washing smuggled on a good day; messages, letters, these notes. Daniel and Mark are old enough to be of help to their mother, which is good; but also old enough to realise what is happening to us and what will probably be our fate. Tony is four and may be distracted by the games that Rachel organises with the other mothers. Marie was born into this distorted world of the Occupation and the persecution of our people. In her second year on this earth, what can she possibly know of normal, sane life outside the reach of her mother's arms?

What more could I have done? The Union générale des israélites de France was our main means of negotiating with Vichy and the Nazis — with limited cards in our hands, my eloquence and guile worn thin as the roundups and selections gathered pace.

I have played the King in this infernal game of sacrificing pawns; a strategy to win time and lives. Though the end-game was always clear before us, if we chose to see it — there was never any chance of escape. There has been so much talk of routes to Spain, Portugal, clandestine meetings, shady contacts and hollow promises. And who is to say that some of those might have achieved as much or more than my negotiations?

Is it not possible to understand that one may be French and a Jew? That one does not exclude the other? In the cemeteries at the Front the graves of comrades are lined up together, without distinction of rank or race or religion or blood. The unity of nation was surely sealed by their sacrifice. A lack of intelligence, a lack of imagination is the fault here.

The tragic fault. A Frenchman may fight for his country, distinguish himself at Chemin des Dames in the worst of the fighting, with fixed bayonets driving the Hun back and stepping over the corpses of his men and comrades. After that bloody Easter rising out of our trenches — men refusing to leave our trenches, some going down with "wounds" to their feet, shrapnel and bullets, Pétain took over and quelled the mutiny; we were close to anarchy in that mess. Pétain — a hero and then a fool: our General and then the Marshall. Perhaps a traitor?

I am a true Frenchman who has been reduced to throwing accusations at his country. My Croix de Guerre for the action at Craonne: Daniel and Mark have played with that medal, my badges and helmet. All that left behind at Les Milles with their innocence. A man's family is what is really at the centre of his being.

The guards here could have been men in my company, saluting me and putting their trust in officers. Scratching their names in the walls of the cave before our attack. The pair standing now at the entrance to our block turn away, smoke with a serious indifference, do not make unnecessary eye contact. They are once more French pawns in a German game. Each survives in his own way.

These buildings should have been the homes of the bright young things — doctors, lawyers, officials with their first foot on the ladder. High, bright and modern in the Seine-Saint-Denis above an old dame of a city. Instead, women and children and old men die each day under on the straw strewn across the concrete floors of this unfinished place — a complex of apartments grafted onto an old Paris suburb. Drancy was to have been the shape of the future in this city, the beginning of life in a new decade. Standing at the unglazed window gaps it is possible to hear the street sounds of Paris going about its crippled business. And that is the most painful poem, the most jarring étude: La Cité de la Muette.

As the trains come and go, emptying the place of its unwelcome guests, Paris remains silent, this place will become a silent, empty accusation. Drancy will be a shameful memory, best forgotten.

March 11th, 1944

I.

Smoke in the Paris sky.
The thick reek of flesh like bad pork
in the evening air.
Gouts of smoke from 21, rue le Sueur
in the sixteenth arrondissement.
Flecks fly-blown on the window-panes,
smuts on this morning's washing.
Heavy, drifting slowly, the smells infect the streets.
The butcher closes his door,
the grocer waves his apron
like a housemaid shooing at cats,
the butcher's nostrils flare.

The Gestapo's basement window slams shut.
In the Bar Balzac on the square
a man turns away and hunches back to his card game –
he needs a Queen –
picks up his pluming Gauloises
and fills his lungs.
Turns over the Jack of Spades.

II.

Lucien – a cognac,
a cognac, large – now!

....63845...

Hello? Hello?

Put me through to Ducet…

Bonjour, Officer Teyssier… I'm at the Balzac…
Sixteenth… send a car to number twenty one rue le Sueur…
The occupant is Dr Petiot, Marcel Petiot….
Homicide, yes… bodies… an abattoir… all kinds of shit, I tell
     you,
a stove in the basement still going strong….
Christ… there's a woman's hand stretched out of the door… in
     the ashes.

The Fire Chief forced an entry… smoke… yes…
his men are puking like girls, all over the place.
I tell you – this is something big, for the Chief to deal with
     himself,
maybe even the Commissioner… the Gestapo?
I suppose so.
A man came by, the owner's brother, he said.
He said they were pimps and collaborators from the Boche
     whorehouse
round the corner… no… no… he said he was Resistance,
so we let him make off.

Hello? Hello?

Ah!

Lucien, give me that bloody drink, quick!

III.

Bonjour colleagues, mes amis.
I should do no more at this point than read the open file on the
    Valéry/Petiot case:

Nine severed heads floating in the Seine.
A dozen parcels of human remains
carved and broken like chickens.

A side of ribs and an arm complete.
Each face and scalp peeled off in a piece.
(Fish could not have done that, it is an expertise
of one of the master butchers.)

Finger-prints, too, stripped off like old paint.

A man came close to capture when
he was seen to throw a woman's hand off the Pont de Passy
on to a passing barge.
The stream of bodies stopped some months past.

What worried us most was the murderer's habit
of using thighs as pin-cushions.
We are told that this is a not uncommon practice
among students and practitioners of medicine,
while they light a cigarette
or scratch their nose over a cadaver.

Then again, the bodies at rue le Sueur
had thighs marked thus.
The property, one of many it seems, was owned
by Dr Eugène Petiot
for the suspect has been known by these various names:

this man is quite obviously a shifter of identity, slippery, and a person of whom we should be wary and vigilant.

***

I also have on our files the following report:

A close examination of the subject's personal history reveals three of the four childhood symptoms of a psychotic personality:

Sonambulism; enuresis and defecation; and cruelty to animals.

From witnesses in Auxerre we have –

At five the boy Petiot became attached to a neighbour's kitten. He would hug the cat in a loving embrace. But one day the maid found the boy scalding its paws in the boiling wash. Remorseful, that night he took the kitten to bed with him. But in the morning the limp creature was discovered under his pillow, smothered.

It is recorded that the boy also stole young nestlings and poked out their eyes with a pin. Thus blinded, they blundered around on the kitchen table, bumping into each other while he laughed. He placed them back in their cage and they battered themselves senseless against the bars, to his further amusement.

We take this to be proof of a psychopathic character, though another transgression – arson – was not apparently remembered at this stage. The young Petiot burned nothing. That would be later.

IV.

Now the music comes to an end and we may begin.
We have lit the candles of reflection,
the room is secure and when we take each other's hand
the circle will be complete and the channels will be open…

We are gathered in the house of truths and visions.
Fix your thoughts.

Friends, I find him.
Loosen your hands and turn the palms upwards to the light,
as I do now.

I see dark rooms away from the blinding sun.
I see wall hangings.
I see long, flowing robes.
There is the smell of cooking,
the noise of market traders,
the sound of an animal – a goat?
A strange, dry cough in the long throat –
it is a camel.
This tells me Africa.

I hear you, I hear you.
Alright, I will try…
Yes, Morocco –
It is Morocco where Petiot hides,
a boat from Marseilles across to Africa.

My feeling is that he will escape
all that they will do.
He is beyond any of them.
The power can be light or dark,

For he changes from one to another –
he is our enemy, and our brother,
for in this life, for now, in these days,
we do not distinguish and he is carried in many.

Georgette Petiot

Interview by Commissaire Georges-Victor Massu, Police Headquarters, March, 1944.

Madame Petiot, you will answer my questions fully and with total honesty. These are matters of the most serious weight and you have been made fully aware of our findings at your property 21, rue le Sueur in the Sixteenth arrondissement.

'It was never my property. My husband and I had several properties and that is one which I did not visit. I knew nothing of the place. Perhaps I went there once – a large and unpleasant house, dark and in need of much work, I think.'

And on the day of the discovery of the crimes in that place, what were your movements, your husband and you?

'I do not…'

It was on the eleventh of March. A Saturday.

'Yes, well, we would have eaten lunch, but it was interrupted by a phone call. Marcel has many doctor's calls at all hours. Such a popular and busy practitioner. But this time I saw him return to the table with a very serious face. "It is the police," he said. "Some problem at rue le Sueur. I will have to go and take care of it. Nothing to worry about." And then he got up and took his coat. When he did not return after several hours, I became worried and imagined that perhaps he had been picked up by the Germans and who knows what?'

Did you make telephone calls or in any other way try to discover what might have happened?

'Well, no. You know how it is in these times. I felt that it was best to keep it to myself. I thought perhaps he might have taken off to

Auxerre where our son is at school. For safety, Gérard, our boy, is staying there with my sister and going to school there.'

But by the following day, Sunday, you say you still knew nothing?
'On the Sunday I decided that I would go to Auxerre to be with my son and to see whether his father had gone. I went to the Gare de Lyon to catch the first train. It was very early, seven thirty, I think, and then I found that there were no trains.'

But, of course, it was a Sunday. That must have slipped your mind. With your being so concerned and upset…
'Yes, that was it. So…'

So, you waited another whole day and did nothing?
'I went to church to pray for him. And then returned to the waiting room of Gare de Lyon hoping – I do not know what I was hoping for, but that is where I saw a newspaper and read about the terrible things they said that my husband had done.'

And did you report to the police to clarify things? No, you ran away.
'That is not it. I spent the night, most of it, sitting on the stairs of a building my husband owns on the rue de Reuilly. I don't know why. I couldn't think of what else to do. Then I went to a restaurant on the rue de Bercy before I caught the evening train to Auxerre.'

And no Marcel Petiot was there. Of course. And no-one knew anything about him. Of course. The hotelier on rue de Bercy, the Hôtel Alicot, has corroborated that bit of your story. He also knows your brother-in-law Maurice Petiot quite well. You Petiots are connected all over the city, it seems.

And did you know that your brother-in-law was witnessed many times at the murder house just before our discovery of the bodies? Maurice, the haulier, the odd-job man, the probable accomplice to those murders? Part of the Petiot team?

'There was no team. Maurice was kind and offered to help with Gérard and his new schooling arrangements at Joigny. That's what I know.'

Ah, yes, the change of school for the boy. What difficulty he will now face when he carries this scandal with him to that school and for the rest of his life.
'A mother. I only… I can…'

Dear God, the woman is fainting. Right. Stop the interview.
    You, send for someone. See to her, will you?
    And then get her out of my sight.

Georgette Petiot: interview conducted, but no significant information or material coming forth. The loyalty of a wife. Or the ignorance of a woman in a man's affairs. Perhaps a well-rehearsed performance. Attractive woman of a certain age. In the right lighting she could be an actress, hair styled, pearls and several dress rings – there has been no shortage of money for her. A performance which ended in tears. Unlikely to crack with further interrogation. Will play the woman's card. Recommend efforts directed at other players in this game. The brother, neighbours, professional contacts. The criminals whose names come up – drugs, prostitution. Dangerous areas – care must be taken.

Witness Statements, April, 1944

Professor Victor Avenelle, no 23, rue le Sueur, Professor of Romance Language and Literature, the Sorbonne:

On several occasions I had heard what could be taken to be muffled shouts, screams even, all from number 21. These were invariably in the late evening, just before midnight. I did not investigate these noises, nor did I report them to the authorities. Which authorities? It is not unusual in these times to hear and see things which before the present situation would certainly occasion comment, alarm even. I have my work, you see, my work which occupies me above everything else. Our literature is now, surely, more important than ever: France will survive by its culture when all else fails.

Madame Jacques Mercier, no 22, housewife:

We saw little of our neighbour across the road, though he had bought the house some two years before, I think. Was he a doctor? We had a princess, you know. Real quality, though I think she used the place to store her things and never really lived there. Yes, I have heard cries for help in the distance, it seems. My husband sleeps like the dead and snores, so often I am awake. He has become quite deaf. The cries were always between ten and midnight and did not last long. Then silence. We are a short road between avenue Foch and avenue le Grande Armée and there is little by way of cars and lorries. The footsteps, a cry, the squeak of a bicycle.

Count de Saunis, no. 23.

I have heard noises. Screams coming from no.21. Who knows what happens these days? It is no secret that we are a few streets away from the Gestapo and the Milice. It is better not to get involved. At Christmas time last year there was a banging and noise of building work. A man, dark-haired, would come and go on a green bicycle with a trailer. What he carried was covered by a tarpaulin, but I saw the wooden frames of paintings sticking out. It was not my business. This street used to have a better class of householder. I have considered moving, but...

Mme. Pageot, concierge at no. 23.

The Princess kept herself to herself, so did the doctor. But when work was needed on our wall Dr Petiot was happy to let our workmen enter and go up to the roof. That would have been a year or two back. I remember I had the key for days afterwards as he was not there to have it back from me. He was a gentleman – well, a doctor, of course. Though I did sometimes see him in rougher clothes, as if he were doing work himself and not paying workmen, as one would expect. This has always been a good area. Respectable. Though last summer, in June, I think, there was a truck unloading suitcases and other bags. The doctor was being helped by the man I took to be his brother. So alike in the face. I didn't count them all. I stopped at forty or so. There were so many I thought that no. 21 was being turned into a hotel.

Mme. Marie Lombre, concierge at no.22.

I was not sure who lived there, or what their business was. One understood a doctor, but then what sort of doctor would turn up at all hours on a bicycle and cart wearing a Breton beret like some sort of rubbish man or removals business? Once I heard a horse and carriage and looked out to see an old-fashioned fiacre drawn by a worn-out nag. There were sounds – cries or screams – a woman's, I thought. But in these times some women forget themselves and any sense of decency goes out of the window. One evening, I swear, I heard the popping of champagne corks. Who has anything to celebrate these days.

Georges Redouté

He was my doctor, what can I say? I am a house painter, these thirty years. I respected a doctor. When I did in my shoulder, he was the right man, for sure. Got me back to work. So, when he came to me and needed help... The Resistance, he said, they were keen not to have him taken by the Boche because of all the secrets he had and the things he had done. He had cleared up some mess for his 'friends' and just wanted to stay until things quietened down. You know, things were confused in those days and people moved in the shadows. Even disappeared, some of them...

My place was over in the rue faubourg Saint-Denis, so why would they search there?

When I saw what had happened, what the papers were saying, I took it with a pinch of salt. What can you believe these days? So, anyway, I asked him straight: 'Is it true about the bodies at your place in rue le Sueur?' And he said, yes, it was, but that they were Boche or collaborators and deserved no better.'

The next day we had coffee and I asked him again, 'Swear to me, on the head of your son, that what you say is true and that the newspapers have it all wrong.' He said that he had killed, it was true, but all of them had been enemies of France, traitors and scum the Resistance wanted to see the back of. 'The papers do not know about all the bodies my colleagues and I have thrown into the canal de l'Ourcq and buried in the Bois de Boulogne.' He said that those stories about a secret killing room and a periscope for watching the victims die was all made up stuff to sell newspapers.

He was with me for weeks and was growing a beard to look different. For when he would go out and take up arms again, he said. He was known as 'Special 21' as an agent, and that maybe he would try and make it out to Spain. But that didn't happen...

He called himself Dr. Valéry and got hold of papers to carry it off…

So, when Paris was liberated he was there. He came home – around the 20th, it was – with what he said was the official drum from the place de République. He had a pistol and German hand grenades – I didn't welcome them in the house, I can tell you. 'I took the gun from a mortally wounded comrade,' he said.

He now wore an F.F.I. armband and told how he'd fought at l'Hôtel de Ville, place de la Concorde and the boulevard Saint-Martin, where five of his comrades had been killed. He was scruffy, but looked like a man full of the excitement of war and killing. Quite different from the way he had been when hiding…

Later, I told him he should go now to the police and clear the air about the rue le Sueur business. He said that he understood that his wife and his brother Maurice were still under arrest and he didn't want to cause them problems. 'Best to be quiet and let things go away,' he said. Which I thought was a funny way to go…

Especially when the next day he turned up with a motor car parked outside and saying they'd made him a captain for the F.F.I. in charge of chasing down more traitors and collaborators. God help, them if he catches them, I thought. He did bring me a chicken and some butter: where the hell did he get that? I thought.

But that was the last time. He went back out and I never saw him again. Captain Valéry disappeared and Doctor Valéry too. Didn't see him take his stuff. Not much of it in his room anyway. You have to trust who you know and those that have been straight with you. Which is all you can go on when the world has gone mad. Which it has…

Simone's Rabbit

When the food trucks arrive from the countryside
there is always a line of women.
We are the second sex, we queue for scraps.

My hair's a mess, so I fashion these turbans I wear
to cover the grease and the knots.

My late uncle's greatcoat from Verdun
has become a jacket and trousers for my bike rides.
We make do. We dress à la mode utilitaire.

Jean Paul and I always need another lover to connect,
two in a love that is anchored by a third:
our family's a ménage à trois,

In my dreams she is tall, blonde, uniformed.
At the Café de Flores, her legs stretch out across the cobbles,
she brushes crumbs of croissant off her pressed trousers,
the creases as sharp as razors.

They are tucked into boots of polished black leather
that gleams in the sun.
Her cap badge is an eagle with geometric wings.

Her lovers have their hair coiffured in the salon.
For them there is no shortage of shampoo,
the dryers all function.
In the basement two young men pedal furiously
on fixed racing bikes that generate the heat.

La belle France plays the housewife or the whore,
she smuggles through the checkpoints
explosives in her brassiere, bayonets beneath her skirts.

Our defeated men, our imprisoned men,
need us to be women, and more than women were.

We draw on our legs the seams
of silk stockings that do not exist for us,
that exist only in the imaginations of men.
We are the illusionists,
we are their dreams,
we are the second sex.

Yesterday Jean Paul caught me unwrapping a rabbit
that reeked to high heaven –
rancid as an overhung hare.
He threw it out of the window, raged and cursed the war,
then went out to the café, or the Combat office,
or Michelle, or Louise, slamming the door.

This evening we ate rabbit in a country stew –
garlic and vinegar and mustard disguised the taste.
One of the miracles only a woman can do.

From an Officer's Diaries – 2

*

News from the East came in this morning. It goes very badly, though we must massage the figures of the casualties, men and equipment. As we retreat the Russians feed off us. It is impossible to hobble every tank, fire each fuel supply. When they take the boots off our young men it is said that the frozen feet come away with the leather. A captured Russian Colonel when asked how they had survived and continued their resistance, admitted that they had taken to eating corpses. He insisted that he himself had only partaken of the livers.

*

Went to the first night of Breker's exhibition at the Orangerie which was opened by Bonnard; Aristide Maillot was effusive in his praise, while Sacha Guitry said that if all the statues had shown erections it would have been impossible to walk around the gallery. Certainly, Hitler's favourite sculptor glorifies the male nude in all its Aryan glory. Guitry's films are particularly fine examples of the French cinema, I think.

*

My work does not necessitate dealings with the worst of the French – the Milice, Darnand and those murderous crooks at rue Lauriston. One pays as little attention as possible to the gossip and rumours about body parts in the Seine, evil doctors of death and the disappearances. Of course, there are drugs and abortions. A city which lives in the bright lights of music and dance and art, the theatre of Cocteau, Sartre, Anouilh and Claudel, must needs have its shadows cast in corners, its dark storms of the night. Where there are scraps there will be rats.

*

A fine von Karajan concert last night. Beethoven, naturally. The audience was mixed German and French and the reception was notable for its warmth and camaraderie. Music is a stream which flows across borders and times. Karajan's wife is, I believe, a Jew, but he is a Party member. I could check the papers, but who cares when the music transports one so.

*

Anita writes less regularly now: she is anxious to move away from Berlin and buy us a house in Saxony. It is clear that the bombing raids are becoming heavier and more accurate. Hans may soon be called up to serve and I would wish him to enlist with my old regiment, if possible. Things have gone to horror in the East and with the Americans grouping in England an invasion cannot be far off. The Italians are led by a minor character from a bad opera and will surely be of little use in the south. Here in Paris the band plays on and the wine flows and La Coupole still serves the most exquisite duck – Canard à la presse. Life pressed out of a carcass tastes sublime.

*

On most of my walks I take in the scope of the city: but do not fail to notice the structures – how the limestone from which many houses and the quais are made has those tiny fossil whorls from millennia ago. Artists, writers and generals, we strive to leave some imprint and that the future should read it for what it was meant. Our bombs and those of our foes may merely serve to clear a way for the monoliths of a New York or Chicago.

*

Coffee and cake with Werner at the Café Bonaparte: he is concerned with transport, statistics and planning, and has stayed out of the firing line. One of his brightest young men at the university had been writing to him from the East. He describes the excitement of his unit clearing villages and disposing each one of them, by shots – body after body falling into one mass grave of a pit they bulldoze over. "He was an astute critic of the High Romantic. Such a promising academic," Werner said. "Nothing from him for two months now."

*

One of my walks through the Père Lachaise cemetery: the famous, of course – Chopin, Moliere, Rossini, Apollinaire – and even Jewish and Muslim sections, which are, effectively, undistinguished now. The awful monstrosity that is Oscar Wilde's tomb. This afternoon, a proliferation of butterflies, bees, a blackbird singing. And what if misguided bombs fell here? Or we were ordered to destroy this place along with the other historic sites of Paris? If our endeavour fails and we have to retreat?

*

November 11th: I pause at l'Arc de Triomphe and the flame of the unknown soldier. And he is one of those we killed in a trench at Cambrai when we stormed over from Caudry. Or the Poilu I bayoneted near Diksmuide. There is a bitter east wind which plays with the flame.

Combat

May 7th, 1944
Editorial:

After nearly four years under the oppressive heel of the Nazi it would be tempting to acquiesce, to accommodate the occupying force. We must never do that. Never cease to struggle in whatever way we can – man, woman and child – to oppose the Germans until they are expelled from this land. We have seen our traitors at the very highest level – Pétain and Pierre Laval – Pétain, the hero of Verdun who has forgotten why he fought and why so many of our countrymen were slaughtered; and Laval, who shamefully runs the Vichy puppet-show. French men and women are pressed into labour for the enemy while the weak and marginalised are picked off mercilessly.

They tell you to obey the law and the Milice. The Milice are not the gendarmerie, not the protectors of the law; they are a bunch of crooks, sadists and villains. They plunder us, they torture us, they run wild under their German masters like wolves released in the forest. The Resistance, and all true Frenchmen will at least disobey these crooks, obstruct these crooks and, ultimately, assassinate these vermin.

And as for the wolf-pack masters? Do not be party to their actions and movements. Do not think, "I shall stay low, live peaceably, keep my precious head down, because it will not be forever; this cannot last for the rest of my life." There is no "rest of my life" possible when the Germans decide to enact revenge, punishments for actual and perceived offences. One of their men is killed, murdered or caught in a traffic accident, they will count out five, eight, ten of us and shoot us in front of our families.

Your neighbour bravely gives refuge to another fleeing the authorities: you will be implicated and be shot. The Boche suspect your community is harbouring fugitives, but cannot find them – they will drag out your mayor, your priest, your councillor and put a bullet in their heads. You will wash blood and brains off the cobbles of your street. This is total war and must be answered by total resistance and courage.

Do not read the servile press, the comfortable press, the traitorous press: Combat is an organ of truth, a beacon of light. We report what is actually happening. You can trust us, for without trust there is no victory over evil.

Just two weeks ago we learned of another of their atrocities. Patriots exploded two devices on the railway line passing Ascq to our north when a SS Panzer Hitlerjugend deployment was derailed. It is believed that none of these bastards was killed – more's the pity. Nevertheless, these animals dragged dozens of men who lived each side of the track from their homes and families and executed them. Railway staff were also shot. These are the curdled cream of Hitler's nation, poisoned young men, Nazi whelps who breathe only hatred, for this German nation is breeding evil upon evil.

Combat knows there will be reckoning: for Ascq and all the other crimes and atrocities. Combat calls for that return to decency and law; Combat will report of that triumph, for it will surely come!

Report on the Eugène/Fourier Resistance Escape Route, May 30th, 1944: Dr Robert Yodkum, Chief, Jewish Affairs Section (IVB) rue des Saussaies

We have made significant progress with our investigations into the escape route for criminals and undesirables run by one "Dr Eugène". The incarcerated Jew Yvan Dreyfus, who we arrested at Montpellier on a previous attempt to cross the border to Spain at Irun has been released from our camp at Compiègne and used as a bait, a "mouton" for the wolves. The barber, Fourrier, is engaged as a go-between linking the fugitives and the escape network which takes them to Spain, Portugal and South America.

We have discovered that payments of around 50,000 francs may be demanded at the point of engaging the services of the organization, with further instalments at various stages of the exercise. Someone purporting to be a policeman escorts them to hotels where they are held at their own expense until moved on. Further members of the gang take them to the station where they pay another large sum. They may take cash but all jewelry and other valuables are left with the gang and returned to them on safe arrival in Spain. It is, of course, impossible to ascertain whether this is in fact what happens.

In the case of Dreyfus, a well-connected and wealthy Jew, there must surely have been special arrangements and fees. Unfortunately, the bungling intrusion of agents from Berger's men from section IV E-3 blew the set-up before the "doctor", the brains of this tawdry set-up, could be apprehended. Interrogation of the barber and several others is proceeding. From their squealing and screams it would seem that we are close to discovering who Dr Eugène really is and where we may find him.

There is no trace of Dreyfus. He has disappeared. He may have reached Spain and be returning to America.

Inspection: rue des Grands-Augustins, 6th Arrondissement, June 1st, 1944
Obersturmfuhrer Otto Richter, SS.

I conducted our scheduled check of the apartment and studio of the Spanish alien, who continues to present no concerns for us. There was no subversive literature and no evidence of association with or support for the Communists or the Resistance. However, the subject arrived late and as we were about to force an entry he let us in. He had been detained at the Catalan Bistro, he said.

He is a man of modest stature and some sixty or so years of age. Whilst showing few courtesies he allowed us full and unhindered access to his apartment and 'studio'. There are stacks of canvases and folders of drawings on paper which are completely in the degenerate style and which do not address concerns with or affect knowledge of the occupation of France and the war. He has even taken to scribbling on match boxes and shaping bread into grotesques. He may be mentally unstable.

There are 'portraits' of women, as far as one may discern, but for the most part his pictures are of banal pots, coffee cups, fruit and lamps on table tops. These are unskilled and misshapen, unrealistic in terms of their form and colours.

Observations:

It is a mystery why this old man should be held in such high regard by the English, French and Americans: good money chasing bad art. Presumably this little man clings to his existence in Paris because a return to Spain would see him strung up by our former ally Franco. There would, however, be nothing gained by our arrest of him and therefore I concur that we leave him to fester in his room among the daubs and scratchings of his febrile brain. We have more important matters to attend to and defend our France against enemy incursions. We found no evidence to connect this man with the underground system suspected of transporting Jews and other undesirables across into Spain.

Nature Morte

Four years, but one survives. Thrives even. Materials have been scarce at times, but canvases may be re-used and Comrades and friends from the Resistance have brought small quantities of metal for maquettes. There is life and society at Le Catalan with Sartre and Camus and Simone still at large. Francoise is a breath of new life and an invigorating muse. I do not grow old. She brings colour to my life and painting.

If my still lifes are so many it is because one spends many hours indoors and the works build up one after the other. How many angles has a coffee pot? How may one eat a pigeon? How good is the smell of fresh leeks from the market with soil still on their roots? My pots are the colour of grey uniforms; my contour lines the colour of jackboots. Whatever I choose to paint, it is resistance to them; art will hurt them as the constant cutting of throats.

Max has gone – they took him at Saint-Benoit-sur-Loire and sent him to Drancy for the trains going east. Pneumonia. They killed him with neglect. His brother and sister before him. The bastards arrested him in the cathedral at mass – Christian by religion, but a Jew by race. Years ago, when he converted, I became his godfather: can you believe that? The Jews have suffered terribly in this war. Max was a Jew and a queer – they would shoot him for the first and hang him for the second.

There was talk of an underground escape route, a house in the Sixteenth, but who knows what is real, actual and what is just rumour and despair? At times it seems that Paris has been turned in to a suburb of Berlin. We are strangers, one to another.

In her apartment Francoise grows tomatoes in a pot. They ripen as the war heightens. Soon we will be liberated. The tomatoes and cherries I paint are to be eaten then.

When their senior SS man came to see me at the beginning

he pointed at Dora's photographs of Guernica.

"Ah, of course, you did that."

"No, you did," I told him.

La Cité de la Muette Infirmary, Drancy
March 1st 1944.

Drancy/March?

My Dearest Pablo,
God know whether this will reach you. I will no longer be here if and when it does. I am racked on a cross of coughing and the toad sits on my chest laughing···

I fear I shall not see another Shabbat, another Sabbath. Now I am prisoner 15872···.

This is hell made manifest in our most beautiful city···madness··· there is no sense, nor has there been for these past years. I had always hoped to die in a Breton landscape — big skies — the sound of the sea against the cliffs, shingle below stirred like snare drums.

The talk here is of these cattle trains taking us to the East to our deaths. Is that what happened to Gaston and Myrthe-Lea? Could you ask about them? Her poor husband too. They were arrested ,then there was no word···I fear the worst. I have no family now. The authorities might listen to you, Pablo.

I am visited by the dead in my dreams — a summer at Tréboul, the sweet English boy Christopher painting my portrait. He was dead before the next summer, not yet thirty, a child, by his own hand. To jump in front of a train···it would be quicker than this···Dear Kit Wood···charming and confused and crazy···

The young guards here are ugly and ageing daily in their evil. They are not even the Boche, but our own, doing the Germans' dirty work. The Milice are the scum of our France tipped out of prisons, dug out of gutters. Their cruelty···

> *Rats who scurry at our feet*
> *Are thrice as jolly, thrice as sweet*
> *As those who strut their booted legs*
> *And turn their backs on those who beg.*

Life is a chariot on a golden beach,
Always driven out of reach...
Sand, shells, hells······

Last night I was with you and Cocteau and Braque and Modigliani again sharing wine and coffee in our room on the Boulevard Voltaire. Before the war that was before this war···Braque made a joke about my Jewish crucifix···we laughed at your unmade bed, the stains of food and women···We were making the world new, weren't we?

Later Christ came to me and took me in his arms. I pray that he may find me again.

There is a kitchen woman here in whom I glimpse some humanity, I think. I am giving her this letter in trust, in extremis···

Love to you and Dora
and all the artists and poets···
As ever,

Max

September 1974, Port Lligat, Spain

The wily old Spaniard conned me at the opening of his museum in Figueres. Torrential rain that evening and when Dali made his entrance he was dressed like an emperor. The crowds parted. On the stage he called for me and embraced me and then extolled the qualities of my bust of Cocteau which he had borrowed for the museum. "My friend Herr Arno, Germany's greatest sculptor, welcome. How kind of you to donate this magnificent work to the collection." Thus it was that the loan became a "gift". Who could resist Dali the magician, the showman?

I stayed with him at Port Lligat where he had the most beautiful house with the most beautiful views across the bay and hinterland. Seductive. Across these lands he has imagined processions of people and creatures, elephants on stilts, clocks that bend to the shape of the rocks, all under the relentless gaze of the Spanish sun.

My commissioned bust catches him with those extravagant, proud moustaches like aeroplanes taking to the sky. And his hair as I saw it blown by the wind off the sea. It is the hair of a madman, but, then what great artist is not mad?

How remarkable that this southern edge of Spain should produce two major artists – Dali and Picasso. Two geniuses so different in their visions and skills.

I knew Pablo in Paris entre deux guerres; those cafés with Modigliani, Cocteau and Kahnweiler. We saw to it that he was left alone during our occupation. Degenerate art, but too significant to be cut off at the throat.

At the Figueres museum opening the thing that struck me most deeply was a Dali still life of a breadbasket and a cut loaf. Simple and profound. Pablo during our occupation of Paris, I think, painted many such still lifes. And, of course, his women. We could hardly object to that, but I see now that a bowl of fruit, a lobster and loaf of bread may be as powerful as a grenade.

From an Officer's Diaries – 3

*

On a bench in the Tuileries I looked up to see more bombers than ever before: a murmuration of starlings. They are passing over on their way to Germany. Reports that after one week's raids Hamburg suffered over 30,000 dead and almost 100,000 injured. They are using phosphorus now as well as the H.E. More are dying of burns and asphyxiation than from explosions and shrapnel. Here they are still attacking the outskirts and some railway lines, but we lead a charmed life in the City.

*

Last month D introduced me to Georges Braque and I am now a visitor to his studio. Braque, like Picasso, seems to be working on a small scale – the still life. La Saucière a table with lemons, a glass and a fork, the whole thing tilted towards us as if asking where now in these blue shadows? Then small bronzes of a Cavalier, horses that gallop into the wind with pointed heads like the noses of aircraft. In a time of chaos and bestiality is it surprising that man turns to the classics in form and principle? The figure and simple objects.

*

Bombs by the English last night hitting the outskirts of the city and, specifically, the Renault factory: a dozen or so of our dead and nearly a hundred French workers. Explosives, like music, cannot discriminate.

*

The purge has reached Paris and some of my friends and superior officers have gone, including Stülpnagel. Hanged or garrotted, as is the little painter's fashion now. That he should survive the bomb thanks to a brutally formed concrete table in that bunker. In Paul's second letter to the Thessalonians: "And for this cause God shall send them strong delusions, that they should believe a lie." It seems that I am to survive, for the moment. Thus, I could not resist a visit to Avenue de Lowendal where Bernasconi had bound for me two volumes of the Catalogues Coleopterorum. There is solace to be found in my shared etymological endeavours with a deceased German Jew: subtiles, beetles, bees, ladybirds, survived the first war and will survive the present. Yesterday afternoon in the Bois I found two red scarabs of particular interest. There is, no doubt, a cornucopia of nocturnals, but there has been Maquis and gangster activity there at night, so one has to be cautious.

*

Bodies have been found burning in a basement in the 15th. A few streets away from one of my booksellers on rue Lauriston – last week when I called he had kept for me a *Dictionnaire de la Langue Verte: Argots Parisiennes Comparés* by Delvau, 1868; an unexceptional binding. The disappeared do not concern us as there were no reports of our soldiers among the dead. It's a civil matter which it suits us to have the Gendarmerie deal with. They will have much clearing up to undertake when things have moved on. When we have moved on. Language outlives the body: my Delvau informs me that "Donner cinq et quatre" is to give someone a double slap across the face: the first with fingers and thumb – cinq, and then back with the open palm – quatre.

*

I now recall another instance of burning bodies. In '41 when we threw out the Russians and took over their embassy at 79, rue de Grenalle, l'Hôtel d'Estrères, we discovered a wing which held what must have been execution chambers and a furnace for the disposal of bodies; soundproof walls, electrically operated steel doors, execution spy holes and a bathtub for the cutting up of bodies – a diabolical work of art and engineering. Similar facilities have been discovered in their embassy in Berlin at 11, Litsenburgerstrasse. The rue le Sueur killer may have been tutored by the Communists. Whatever we may have done, regrettable and black deeds, I concede, we may be lauded for our opposition to the savagery of the Russians.

*

The Caucasus, Italy and now the landings in Normandy: things are sliding away from us and the future is bloody and certain. Their bombers have targeted the bridges around the city. The F.F.I. are openly mobilizing. Our troops are wiring explosives through many significant buildings. Here in the Majestic, there is little real coffee to be had. The staff grow surly.

*

Had dinner with F for probably the last time. She is calm and has that depth of understanding and empathy which make some women so special. A bottle of Moet while listening to Mendelssohn. Moments in which the brain takes photographs that may be lost but which will not fade.

*

The irony of a quiet walk back along the Left Bank, the book dealers, bric-a-brac and print stalls locked tight. Just like any other night. And will the Yanks and Tommies patronise them? Will they understand what they will have taken? What this city really means?

*

La Ville Lumière. Le Roi Soleil said, 'Let there be light.' And Paris has sparkled and shone for two centuries. And for two centuries after we have gone.

The city is a lady and smiles on the victor.

Frenchmen!

Citizens, this is the most critical time for your city. You cannot know what killing and destruction the advancing troops of the British and Americans will bring to Paris.

Have we not had four peaceful years of civility under German governance? Do not risk the violence and hatred of our shared civilized values, out European cultures entwined in history.

We are still the keepers of law and order in Paris – do not be seduced by the lies of the Communists who would seek to sway you to their false promises. Continue to resist the savages of the east – Stalin would burn this city to the ground. We are not brutes.

Continue to observe our laws and abide by our civilized values and we will ensure that whatever happens, Paris will be secure for the families, women and children, your way of life. We shall not blow up your bridges or your historic monuments, we shall not destroy what we all respect as the qualities of Paris. French and German blood need not flow in the streets.

All true Parisians should defend themselves against terrorists, preserve order and calm, remain loyal to our shared values of civilization.

Pass this leaflet on to your neighbours and friends.

Commander of the Wehrmacht of Greater Paris.

July 10th, 1944 Confidential and urgent message from Reich Fuhrer Adolf Hitler to General der Infanterie Dietrich von Choltitz, Governor of Paris.

****IS PARIS BURNING YET?****

****PARIS MUST BE DESTROYED.****

Trent Park, Middlesex, December 1944 – March 1945
Transcripts of secret recordings made by MI9

Edited no. 6: General von Choltitz:

…Of course, there are things which I regret. Perhaps also my fellow officers. We all share the guilt. We went along with everything, and we made the mistake of taking seriously the Nazis. We should have dismissed them: "To hell with you and these nonsensical ideas and beliefs."

But we didn't. It was war and I was party to my soldiers acting on such beliefs and misguided principles. I feel ashamed of myself. Perhaps we officers bear even more guilt than those – yes, I shall say it – uneducated beasts. The upstart Hitler wanted to raze Paris. He wanted nothing of that city and its history and culture to survive. It was pointless and vindictive. I could not do that. I did not carry out those orders of a madman. We and the French are civilized peoples, unlike some others, lesser nations and lower peoples. Paris is like a beautiful woman; when she slaps you, you don't slap her back.

…I do regret the distasteful business with the Jews. These acts were not what a soldier trained for or should have engaged in. The little Austrian corporal and his gang got above themselves and lost their way.

…At least here we prisoners are with our own kind. The British are gentlemen and treat us as equals, don't they? The food is decent, the grounds pleasant enough until one reaches the barbed wire. Understandable.

Lord Aberfeldy, our Welfare Officer is, as they say, 'a decent chap'. He talks of having an estate in Scotland, with deer and salmon streams. Perhaps if we had had better fortunes, and the war had gone another way, we could have taken over such estates for ourselves. Here at Trent Park there is little sport, so close to London, or what we have left of it. The Luftwaffe is rarely seen now, though. …We have other means, as you say: the Kirschkern flying bombs are cherries for all seasons, I think. But it's too late a harvest, I fear.

… certainly, as 'guests' of the British we are here in the footsteps of royalty and the famous – Charlie Chaplin and Churchill himself. Two clowns…. The family were Sassoons, I gather, Parisian Rothschilds. Jews, of course. Though the Baronet served in the First War, it seems. And a cousin of his was one of their poets. You were at Diksmuide, weren't you? Despite everything, one has a lasting respect for those in the opposing trenches, shallow, inadequate places. They died bravely and foolishly on our wire, didn't they?

…stew again. Though last week was memorable, you missed that. We were taken under armed escort to lunch at Simpson's on the Strand. Have you heard, Aberfeldy promises the Ritz in Mayfair? Then Saville Row. Probably those gifted Jewish tailors we miss at home.

…After this is all over, as I have no doubt it will be, I would wish to return to Paris. I spent little time there and was much concerned with my duties. I shall plan to stay at the Hôtel Le Meurice, my old headquarters. And get to know once more the City of Light, the city I saved.

Bastille Day, July 14th, 1944

Everywhere I go, it seems, the streets are coloured red, white and blue – France is returning to her true colours and the liberation of this city must be very close. Shop windows, the scarfs and ties people are wearing – it's all the colours of our national flag. It's an open defiance.

For the past four years we have been whistling La Marseillaise in defiance from balconies, alleys, around corners, under our breath: now it is audible and proud on so many lips.

In the Place Maubert there are hundreds – students from the Sorbonne, workers, housewives, children – singing and waving flags, some hidden for these past years, others made from whatever cloth is to hand.

When the gendarmes arrive they are pushed back by some and embraced and exhorted to join in by others. There are no Germans. And now when we see their trucks moving west to the invasion front there are thinly disguised boos and cat-calls. These young men are surely being driven to their deaths. The city is being emptied of Germans: France is being emptied of Germans.

Can it be long before we have a mobilization générale and the people will rise to take over their city, as in 1870?

And then, I saw at the Porte de Vanves, people had dragged out old furniture, boxes, papers and bags – a bonfire was started and it burned for two hours. A straw-stuffed effigy was thrown into the flames. The face was crudely drawn, but it was clear for all to see that it was Hitler. Hitler was burning in the City of Light.

The Final Actions

Jean-Paul and I returned to Paris in late July. Our friend Éluard's poem still holds true:

> Paris is cold and hungry
> Paris no longer eats roast chestnuts in the street
> She wears old, borrowed clothes
> She falls asleep in the stuffy Metro
> Riding to nowhere

A matter of days later the insurrection began and it was clear that the city was in a very dangerous state. One morning when I went out in search of food within a short walk of our apartement I saw young boys and old men fishing in the Seine in the sunshine as if nothing was amiss. Some other boys dived from the bank and swam. This could be a painting by Seurat or Monet. But close by, taking cover behind the balustrades there were FFI gunmen. Then, turning the corner I saw in the Place Saint Michel a German tank seemingly abandoned. Like an old water cistern.

The Party has posted notices across the city – *For Every Parisian, a Boche!*

I thought of this as I watched two young, blonde soldiers who could hardly hold their rifles. And with them, an old man in his fifties who has probably seen action in the First War: he'll die in this one, I thought. They turned the corner and came in view of the partisans crouching by the balustrades. I heard gunfire. Who are the Germans sending to us now? What state are they in?

I walked on to the butcher Éclair who, it was rumoured, was having a delivery of fresh meat, even beef, it is said. I am sick of pigeons and scrawny trabbits.

It is unlikely that the liberation of our city will bring an end to rationing. Or to pain.

Berlin August 20th 1944 Radiogram

To: Vichy Minister of Justice Gaborde
From: Office of Reichsfuhrer S.S. Heinrich
Himmler

IS THE PRISONER KNOWN AS DR MARCEL PETIOT
THE ASSASSIN OF GESTAPO OFFICERS AND THEIR
FRENCH AGENTS, OR IS HE LIQUIDATING MEMBERS
OF THE FRENCH RESISTANCE AND JEWS?

SUPPLY   INFORMATION.   URGENT.   INFORM   US
WHETHER HE IS WORKING FOR OR AGAINST THE
THIRD REICH.

HEIL HITLER

Hôtel de Ville, August 25th, 1944

General Charles de Gaulle, President of the Provisional Government of the French Republic.

Today let us all rejoice and under no circumstances disguise our true feelings – joy, gratitude, pride – the deep emotion of all our people at the defeat of the Nazis in Paris and the return to France of its dearest capital city.

These are memorable and sacred times, times that will define all our lives and that of France itself. Our city has been ravaged, looted, sullied by the occupier. But we have triumphed! You have triumphed! As in our truest hearts we all believed that we would. France in her heart never failed in her belief.

All those true Frenchmen who resisted the enemy and fought back against his many injustices and crimes – all will rejoice this day in the moment of liberation. A liberation achieved by the bravery of our people and the resilience of the French Army and the help also of our allies.

The true Frenchman has done his duty. But here today I have to say to you all that the Boche is not finally beaten. We have scourged Paris of the German, but he must be driven on and out of France and the other occupied countries, our allies.

And there will be a reckoning for the crimes of the occupier. Nothing will be forgotten. Nothing will be forgiven. There are days of reckoning to come, I promise. But let us stand tall and as one on this most magnificent day.

Strengthened by this victory on the streets of Paris our heroic Forces Françaises de l'Intérieur, with new weapons and ordnance, will press on and pursue the enemy into Germany itself. Our brave army has landed in the south and, as I speak, they are advancing up the Rhone valley. France and its forces will unite and will not cease in the conflict until complete victory, complete freedom is ours!

These are days of national unity: we must work together as one nation, one body, one heart and mind. Long live France!

The Ritz Hotel, August 25th 1944.

All the way from the beaches, for weeks that crazy bastard kept talking about coming here and 'liberating the Ritz'. Dodging and weaving our way between the Kraut lines like it was the Wild West.

I figured from the start that he wasn't no real officer. Though he seemed to parley with Patton like they had been at West Point together. He was sure at home with us in the 4th. Wherever we went along the line and forward through those fucking lanes he lorded it and we got ammo and gas aplenty. Even the French guys went along with it. I guess they were glad to have Americans helping out – even a renegade outfit like ours. Then some of them joined us to make a column for the drive down the Champs Elyseés, quiet as a private road.

Though the bar guy here wouldn't let us in with our guns, not even the boss. Take them back to the jeep, Monsieur, it is not allowed, he says. So we do: some classy joint.

Seems like he'd had the best days of his youth in Paris – hanging out with Scott Fitzgerald, movie stars and famous guys – even that traitorous shit Ezra Pound. Word's out that we have Pound secure and he's going to swing or be shot for being Musso's radio stooge.

Even me and some of the other guys had heard of his books. Famous guys. Alex says he'd read *A Farewell to Arms*, at high school. Most of it. Ol' Papa had seen some real action before this, I guess. Maybe he'll write about us after this one's over. He's supposed to be a correspondent for *Collier's Magazine*, but the typewriter's not been seen much since we landed. Sure, you have to do stuff before you write stuff.

First thing here is, he calls for 'Charley Ritz', who I guess must be the owner. No show. But still we check out the rooms and liberate plenty of bottles from the cellar, seizing a couple of men who were hiding down there – not Nazis, probably stooges or collaborators. Anyway, they've gone. Don't ask. Some of the Resistance guys let off rounds on the roof – it was just sheets flapping, but you have to be sure. There's still Kraut snipers about. Booby traps too.

It's champagne for everyone and Martinis by the dozen so the bar tab must be reaching Wall Street figures. Our man will pick it up. He says. Tonight, Jimmy and me are going to bed down in a room that was Goering's or Goebbels's – top Nazi bastards.

Papa's still in the bar, while we've got to go outside to clean and re-load, brush down and get ready for when we have to move out. This Ritzy time can't last. The old guy's been reciting poetry over and over: October tombs, leaves, clouds, no gratitude…

We're in a 'dirty trade' he says. Yep. And from tomorrow, or the next day, there's a lot more trading to do.

August 30th 1.a.m. Café Bonaparte

Jimmy: What a night! What a fucking night! Madness!

The French are mad with joy, Ginger over there doing his party trick juggling with those grenades is madder than ever, the crazy bastard – the wine and the bubbly is flowing and the mademoiselles are so, so grateful! What did I tell ya, Sid?

Sid: You told me, my friend, and did I not believe you? The whole way up here, faces down in the sand and grit at Utah Beach. Up to our armpits in thorns and blood at Caen. And me just dreaming of the Can-Can and the Eiffel Tower and the grateful ladies of Paris.

Jimmy: Bull-shit! You was thinking of nothing but surviving that hell-hole and getting through to the next day. Like we all was. Tubby Barton's IVth Infantry – the Ol' Ivy's Steadfast and Loyal. So we made it, didn't we?

Sid: Ok. True enough, the IVth came through. But when they pulled us out of Falaise and sent us north we knew there were better times ahead.

Jimmy: It opened up, for sure. Flat countryside. And when we passed through the Italian Gate into the city and the flowers and kisses and cheers started…

Sid: And the odd Kraut sniper.

Jimmy: And the odd Kraut sniper – which was dealt with by Anderson's mortar, Anderson's trusty tube, his 'little pussy' – then we knew the good days were back, buddy!

Sid: Ok. But how fucking crazy is this? Where have all the Germans gone. Eh? And guess who's going to have to chase 'em all the way back to the sausage factory? And who and what can you trust here? What's been booby-trapped? Who are all those guys driving the baker's vans and coal trucks with FFI chalked on the side? Taxis with guns poking out of all the windows. Some guy driving a big white British limo. Who are the good guys here?

Jimmy: Guess you've got to trust to your instincts and keep your eyes wide open. And cover our backs.

Sid: Not sure about those dames we saw with the shaved and bleeding heads. A couple of them carrying kids. What's that about?

Jimmy: That, my friend is justice, revenge and just being a sadistic bastard, all wrapped into one. It ain't pretty. But that is what you get when you start a war. Which, let me remind you, was Fritz's big idea.

Sid: But these are the French doing it to their own.

Jimmy: Broads: you fuck the enemy: you become the enemy. Times of war, anything's, everything's for sale. That film actress broad Arletty says, 'My heart is French, but my ass is international.' All bets are off for the duration. Which duration is now at an end for this city. Plenty of friends to fuck now, anyway.

Sid: Like that sleaze-bag trying to sell us an old drum this morning. Guaranteed Napoleon's, for sure. Looting their own stuff, I bet.

Jimmy: What d'ya want – drums, Nazi flags, Mausers? Plenty of guys selling their own sisters and wives. These folks look like they're starving. K Rations and smokes will get you more here than they did in England, I reckon.

Sid: I am wasted. Wasted. Let's get Ginger away from that bar before he blows the whole fucking place to pieces. Ginger, you Louisiana cracker! I have liberated a fine bottle of cognac, my good buddy, and we will retire to our accommodation to chew the fat. And sleep.

Jimmy: How ya gonna keep us down on the farm now that we've seen Paree? Two, three, four... How ya gonna keep us... C'mon, Ginger, you crazy, dangerous bastard!

At rue des Grands-Augustins

Now I am like a circus ring-master. It is all noise and people coming and going and lights and laughter. Because we are free and we have been freed from the Germans.

Now I am like a saint they come to worship. G.I.s litter the floors of my apartment. But they do bring chocolate and cigarettes and tinned meat. My Thursday audience with the G.I.s. Ilès Sassier and her husband try to guard my stairs, but are often overwhelmed.

The wonderful American Lee liberated me. So tall and blonde, but she could not stay to be anointed.

Hemingway arrived like a loud storm. Bourbon, cigars, a box of grenades "A present for my friend Picasso". The next day he presented me with what was left of an SS uniform he said he'd pulled from the body of a Boche he'd killed. A story teller. He is a bull of a man – I held a painting like a cape and could have finished him with my sword as he passed by.

Now I am a master unsated by his harem, a constant line of new nubiles at the door.

I can cut a woman in half, keep one for now and one for tomorrow. It is Pablo's magical disappearing cabinet – the door opens – it is Marie-Thérèse, it closes. It opens again and Dora emerges as if from the waves at Antibes. It closes. It opens and out strides Françoise: in one turn of the light she is a young man of exceptional strength; in another she is lit by a deep womanly beauty. I am drawn to the two faces in a person.

Some days are so dark that even the paint cannot light the way out of these times…

My big exhibition opens in two months. What will they make of my war years?

Woman in a hat with Flowers… Lady with Artichoke… Woman washing her Feet… The Charnel House… Buste de Femme.

An R.A.F. officer visited, an English poet, who said that that we artists have the job of holding a line against the chaos that swirls around. We agreed the city is liberated, but the war swirls round Europe and sucks away one's breath. He said that the war was not fought for the likes of us, but for the poetry and art that comes through us.

Now I am officially a Communist. The Party is perhaps the best way forward through this mess. For the people.

My stashed store of soap and gold has kept safe in the attic wardrobe. One survives.

Lee Miller and the Liberation

Paris in the summer of '44
covering the war and then in the liberated city
a fashion shoot for *Vogue*:
Marlene Dietrich standing against a Napoleon III door,
her head turned away demurely
from the sunlight streaming in.
She's wearing a coat by Schiaparelli,
floral, ruched, flowing, cord-waisted.

Pablo in his studio on rue des Grands-Augustins
standing with his hand on a sculpture
towering over him, the 'Man with a Sheep'.
'Ah, the first Allied soldier I see is you, Lee,
A beautiful woman is liberating the city.'

And then he's with Paul Éluard at the head of that march
at Pére-Lachaise cemetery
to honour the fallen fighters of the Free French,
who'd read Paul's 'Liberté' from copies
dropped by the RAF to the Maquis.

Maurice Chevalier smiling at me on his balcony,
as if about to break into a routine.
Through it all a song and dance man,
Fleur de Paris,
the great survivor wearing boater and bow tie.

Those kids in front of Nôtre Dame
playing on the burnt-out wreck of a Citroën,
the boy posing in the driving seat;
he'll drive them all the way into the rest of their lives.

That winter was so harsh:
chairs stacked at The Tuileries Gardens,
palaces on Place de la Concorde,
the street lamps, the railings,
the stone lions on guard,
all under blankets of snow,
so that the ruins and the great houses
became bright and clean again.
Gendarmes hunched on corners
against the white like black crows.

And that snow did something to cover over
the Occupation's stains, and who knows
how many of the city's crimes.

The photograph everyone remembers,
not one of mine,
was shot by David Scherman of *Life* magazine –
I'm sitting in that bathtub in Hitler's apartment
at 16, Prinzregentenplatz,
in Munich in the spring of '45.
A picture of the Fuhrer propped against the tiles.

The bathmat is soiled by my combat boots,
the mud of Dachau from this morning
spilling over everything. I'd been there,
a witness to that horror.
That night I'd sleep in Hitler's bed.
Two days later we heard he was dead.

O.S.S. Unit 4: Personal and Declassified for Dispatch
Capt. R. Friedman to USA:
Apt. 6 24th Street, Boston. Mass.

My Dearest Josie and Daniel,
Did Daniel get the trucks I sent? Also, keep an eye out for a small package
which is on its way. Guess what — you'll smell sweeter than ever when
you get this special present···

···Now that things are at an end, I am able to write more fully and
share some of the things. I've seen and done over here. Germany, I can tell
you, is wrecked. The whirlwind has come down on them. I do not see them
rising again.

There have been many things along the way which I'll not speak of.
War is a dirty business and though I've been behind the scenes in intel-
ligence work (I can say that now) there's been ugly stuff···

I'm being posted back to Paris tomorrow. There is so much still to sort
out back there, a real backlog. Not the least being the French! They can
be tough guys to deal with. And they've got a lot of clearing out to do.

At the end of last year there were a couple of remarkable things. First,
we debriefed one of our agents. A woman we'd known only as 'the goat
woman'. She'd been behind Kraut lines in France as an organiser and
liaison with the French Resistance fighters. You can bet how much the
Gestapo were keen to get her. 'The limping woman' they called her. Well,
your guy had the honor of meeting her — in the Ritz Hotel, no less —
and turns out she's a younger woman, finely dressed, despite her wooden
leg! Not a goat in sight. And a Radcliffe girl too. Maybe class of '27, before
your sister Martha. They are going to give her a bunch of medals.

And talking of legs — the last day in Paris before I was posted on,
guess what? A damp, dreary day and two guys in army coats and caps
walking across the Place Vendôme in front of me when one of these guys
starts to dance along the side-walk and gutters while the other guy claps
in time. Like a movie or something. USO guys···I thought they must have
been well juiced.

When I get in the foyer of the Ritz the check-in clerk takes their coats

off and the dancing guy turns out to be Fred Astaire. I kid you not —
Fred Astaire. So later I got him to sign my menu card and that's wrapped
around the Chanel I've posted.

You can call that the story of the legs in Paris···

This war in Europe never ceases to amaze and astound. But I sure am
ready for that furlough. My little Dannie's drawings are so cute··· Please
keep sending them on to me.

Big hugs for you guys···.

Dick

IWM (BU 1292)
Memoirs of a British Intelligence Officer: August 1944 – June 1945

From the day we flew in, a matter of weeks after the liberation, in mid-August, and then entered Paris, what followed was a play that lurched from farce to horror and back again. Making contact with and going on 'patrol' with members of the F.F.I. in the suburbs was unnerving. They were little more than a gang of thugs and hooligans, youths and young men and some women who were intent on revenge for collaborative crimes – real and imagined or reported – and lining their own pockets: cash, jewels, portable valuables of any kind.

This sort of anarchy would have been the norm if de Gaulle had not arrived like a school beak to bring things to order. De Gaulle had never liked the English, though we had saved his bacon; perhaps because we had saved his bacon. And housed him for the last four years. He was an obstinate, difficult character, but that is what France needed at this point, a beak with a cane held behind his back. As they processed down the Champs-Élysées, while Churchill waved his hat to the crowds the general was severe, upright and focused on the job in hand. Someone had to sort out the mess, and keep the Communists in check. France could have gone several ways. Which is why we intelligence officers were there from the start.

A few days later I attended a service of thanksgiving at Nôtre Dame, packed with church dignitaries and de Gaulle himself. As the choir filled that huge space with their harmony a shot rang out – a revolver discharged as it transpired by accident – and everyone ducked down or took cover, except, that is, for de Gaulle. A sort of one-man Tour D'Eiffel, he stood over all and embodied the government. The bullet, whether Pétainist, Communist or German would surely have not penetrated that body of conviction, determination and divine right. It was that man's time and France was his.

One evening at the Hotel Scribe we came across Ernest Hemingway, more than one over the odds, who was very, very loud and very, very belligerent. This was particularly disturbing as he had fashioned a large necklace of hand grenades around his neck which fell across his chest. One hoped that they were not primed. Certainly, strange behaviour for one supposedly there as an unarmed war correspondent.

Although our designation liaising with the French intelligence services of the D.G.E.R. was, to say the least, dubious, while in the city our billets ranged from the comfortable to the sumptuous. We were welcomed for tea at the Bristol Hotel where P.G. Wodehouse and his wife were staying in a suite before their arrest. He was never prominent on my bookshelf, but I judged him to be harshly maligned as collaborator for those naïve and ill-timed broadcasts from Germany; a very old man who throughout the war, or any war, for that matter, lived pretty exclusively in a Blandings Estate of his imagination, served, as ever, by his man Jeeves. In the event, one managed to get them out of custody, mainly because the French didn't quite know what to do with them. He'd continued to write his books throughout the whole business and was keen for me to discover if his sales had held up.

There was, indeed, a cast of thousands in that blown-open city: Allied correspondents, agents and officials, Orwell, Philby, Greene, Duff Cooper and Lady Diana. The Coopers soon ensured that the British Embassy, re-instated on the rue St Honoré, became a hub of the highest society in the city, film stars, politicians, Picasso et al.

For me, a stay at the Rothschild mansion on Avenue de Marigny proved strange and strained for me. Victor Rothschild was back in residence and the whole place seemingly had maintained untouched after the Occupation. It had been commandeered by a Luftwaffe general whose taste in and respect for the finer things of European civilization meant that little looting or misappropriation had been perpetrated. The *maître* had remained in charge of the day to day running throughout and, as he said, 'Nazis come and Nazis go, kings and emperors too, but the Rothschilds have seen them all pass by.'

There were a great number of Parisians who had developed a strategy of, or were afflicted by, ennui. So many who had survived, and even prospered, during the Occupation found great difficulty in remembering just where they were on any specific date and where they might have been. The *Épuration* was, I have no doubt, a necessary process for an occupied nation, but the *Légale* was often neglected; men were killed without trial, women, stripped, shaved and publicly humiliated. Whereas Chevalier was soon to be chirping again and Coco Chanel with her free bottles of No 5 handed out to GIs was cloaked in a heady mist of perfume.

One of those justly imprisoned and dealt with appropriately was the crook Lafont, who had run the French version of the Gestapo, with the connivance of the Germans, from rue Lauriston in the 16th. I had the dubious pleasure of interviewing him at the Sûreté. By all accounts, he had lorded it at the head of a collection of gangsters, pimps, hoods and thieves; a brute, a fixer, a spiv, the al Capone of occupied Paris. It was by allowing such underworld people pretty much a free hand during the Occupation that the Germans could run France with so few regular soldiers employed. The Milice and a compliant gendarmerie did their dirty work for them. And, now it was becoming clearer, the elusive Doctor Petiot was an integral part of clearing up the mess.

Lafont was a sorry sight by the time I got to see him; he had been given a taste of his own infernal medicine and bore the scars. The cock of the boulevard with his molls cruising in that infamous white Bentley were a distant memory. His thread-bare suit, no tie, bruised cheeks and scruffy hair spoke of a precipitous fall from grace. He was doomed, of course, the rifles of the firing squad were loaded, the Monsieur of Paris had polished his blade.

Still, he explained, he was sure that his case should be handled by the Allied authorities, as his alleged offences must have been committed during the German rule and therefore were no business of the new French administration. Had he not helped to hide and repatriate RAF pilots and crew who had parachuted over the territory he and his men controlled? Had he not contrived through his Swiss contacts to send food parcels and other luxuries to old friends in England? In common with many others, his argument was that he was constrained and coerced into unnatural actions by the relentless and heartless occupier. I had on the table in front of me a thick file cataloguing his and his associates' widespread criminal dealings that stretched back to years before the outbreak of the war. The man was deluded and thought himself sufficiently clever and eloquent to talk his way out of that dire predicament. It was with little interest, no surprise and a chilled heart that I read of his execution in *Le Figaro* the following week.

I don't ask my lovers for their passport

IN STRICTEST CONFIDENCE
MEMO: Col. Walters to Capt. Jefferies

With regard to Mme. Coco Chanel:

We are not to pursue allegations of collaboration, 'horizontal' or in terms of actual spying. Her liaison with Baron Hans Gunther von Dincklage is well-documented and a substantial file is held in this office. However, both the P.M. and the Duke of Westminster, together with other prominent Englishmen, vouch for her.

It is implied that Chanel may have been involved in highly classified activities between the Nazis and the Allies and should not be apprehended. It is the case that she may already have slipped the net and may have gone over the Swiss border with the Baron.

The Tribunal reports that when asked about her affair with the Baron, she replied, "Really, gentlemen, a woman of my age cannot be expected to look at his passport if she has a chance of a lover."

She was last seen in public in Paris distributing bottles of her No 5 perfume from the front doors of The Ritz to passing American servicemen. These are, indeed, peculiar times. Our files and the French courts are clogged with more pressing matters.

TAKE NO FURTHER ACTION

Beckett's war

I prefer France in war
To Ireland at Peace.

A bench under the trees in the Parc Monceau.
A breeze. Some sun warms the city.
Hold yesterday's paper up before your face.
Signals – the number of pages turned,
which fingers are holding the edge of that page.
The girl on her bicycle circles three times and then
waits at the next bench. For the matchbox you leave behind.
Troop movements. Radio frequency.
Call her Gloria.

&

The priest, being without a use for his prick,
becomes one.

Holy Mother of Judas.
(God).
Judas.
And the good men and women he betrayed
are broken on the broken cross
that is the token at this time we must live and die under.

The priests in both my lands
forever were the worst of their kind.
        Gob shites.
Collaborators as each Christ stumbles from the camp
on a death march.

&

Fingered by the priest,
we are forced to escape from the city.
One step.
      After.
One step.
      After.
Another.

Going south to safety.
Vichy: a border sentry silhouetted against the moon.
East, towards the sea.
Back roads, ditches,
            hedgerows,
fields of heather.
Lying low.
      Forty pieces of silver.

&

The blessing of a cow without the blessing of a pail –
how to accept unannounced gifts,
there being cow shit on the teats, naturally,
and, despite my best efforts, no skill learned from my people
as to the proper directing of the squirt of life
into my held cap.
          So, licking what might have been
from the damp grass. Small things sustain.
Or do not sustain.

She kicks against your leg.

&

And in the next village,
the boulangerie – the memory in the air of that morning's bread,
and pausing to take in the boucher chevalin,
the ample squalor of the opened side of horse,
rich, dark reds and shadows you cannot afford.
Ah, the Cheltenham Races, me boyo.
A long way back. Short odds.

&

The spring, that source, the water which rises
from beneath everything, darkness to light,
the flow from the red strata. You wait for.
Roussillon days: after days after days,
the keeping mum,
                    words
through looks and glances,
the locked-in safety that suffocates,
the keeping of your peace,
the watch your mouth,
                         the trap shut.

&

Post-war St Lô …the sudden scurry of rats
above my head
in the ruins of everything…
and the necessary damage of war…
…rats, impervious to bombing it would appear
not the bodies they feed on…
it is a system a cycle nothing goes
to waste at this time but time
clearing up the havoc…

RÉSISTANCE

Sept. 19th, 1944
Petiot, Soldier of the Reich
By Yonnet

We are reliably informed that the authorities have learned more about
the disappearance of the suspected murderer Dr Marcel Petiot. We are
aware that a deposition has been made to Chief Inspector Massu by a
certain Charles Rolland to the effect that he had known the suspect
during his medical practice in rue le Sueur, but more recently on a visit
that the doctor had not made him welcome and paid him to leave.

In order to escape the attentions of the police and the Gestapo
Rolland had fled Paris and enrolled in the collaborationist militia organisation of the notorious traitor Joseph Darnand. He claimed that he saw

Petiot also enrol and at Pont-Saint-Esprit undertake anti-Resistance training under the Germans. Petiot, claims, Rolland, actually took part in operations against the Maquis. Darnand himself has disappeared and is thought to be with his craven Nazis masters in the Sigmaringen puppet state headed by the Vichy leader Pétain in the soon-to-be conquered Germany. No doubt, these traitors will be taken and receive their just punishment when that ridiculous rat's nest is cleared.

Whatever the truth of this claim, it is clear that Dr Petiot has led a suspect life in these days and that he may prove difficult to catch. A slippery customer who was never to be trusted. Perhaps the horrors discovered at his house in the 16th are not to be avenged or explained before much more investigation.

**Secure Communication to Colonel Roll-Tanguy, Chief of Staff
F.F.I. Forces
September 21st, 1944**

RE: Deployment of Commissioned Officers

Captain Valéry has been based at the Reuilly Armoury and has been effectively active in the struggle against our enemies and those who have collaborated with the Germans. He and his men have both sourced and eliminated several guilty suspects and a considerable cache of money and valuables, including a substantial collection of rare stamps has been brought in to the Armoury. Throughout, Captain Valéry, has been a valued member of the force, leading his men by example.

In considering his application to be re-deployed in the service of France in our overseas territories, I have no hesitation in recommending him wholeheartedly. The DGER service in Indo-China would benefit from his experience, skills and dedication.

I can support his appointment as a Major in the Medical Corps and wish him well in his future service in Saigon. Please sanction this re-assignment, effective from the end of this month: a ship sails for Indo-China at the beginning of November.

Major F. Wetterwald (Dr)

Fetching the bread

I was just coming back from the boulangerie around the corner with rue Lacoste and found the centre of the street filled with a column of German prisoners filing like grey rats from Hamelin. All shapes and sizes. Not the tall, blond specimens that filled our city back in the spring of 1940. They left for the eastern front or Normandy – and death, no doubt – some time back. These had no weapons, no helmets, a bric-a-brac of clothes and shoes and belts. They were unshaven.

Some passers-by and shoppers stared, some hissed and spat. I waited to cross the road and took it all in. These were the conquerors, the authorities that kept us under the boot. These were the cause of our pain and humiliation.

They were policed and herded by our F.F.I. men with some rifles and hand guns, twitching to shoot them if anything happened, any excuse.

And at the tail of this long rat procession, a few stragglers, some limping, some unsteady, with vacant faces and making their way through their own dream. And then scattered among them some so young that they seemed like schoolboys. Some with their hands behind their heads. One kid with his head slumped down against the back of the fellow in front, not looking or taking anything in. What was he thinking of – his mother, his home? What was he remembering?

A few days ago, I thought, I could have slit his throat.

Oct 18th 1944

Sensational letter from Marcel Petiot

By Yonnet

The respected lawyer Mâitre Floriot has brought to our offices a letter from the suspected murderer Dr Marcel Petiot, a man Mâitre Floriot had represented on previous occasions. We must accept the veracity of this document and therefore have agreed to print its claims. Petiot is still alive, and at large, it seems:

I refute the claims made by Rolland and erroneously repeated in your newspaper last month. These were shown to me by a friend, a comrade in the armed struggle to secure the Liberation, who reads your newspaper. The so-called "Charles Rolland" is unknown to me. He is unknown to anyone and is obviously a figment of some fevered imagination. The Police are desperate for results, any results, and are fishing in the Seine and the sewers for any catch.

Petiot has always been a true patriot, having been tortured by the Gestapo, he escaped, assumed a necessary false name and has worked tirelessly for the Resistance cause. He continues to do so and will play his part in avenging the deaths of thousands of his brave compatriots.

At the right moment, when his important work is complete, when France is once again free, he will reveal himself in his true identity and will return to life as a valued medical practitioner, serving the good people of Paris. When tongues and pens are finally freed from their war shackles, there will be witnesses and evidence aplenty to support Dr Petiot; the truth will be revealed and he will be recognized as one of the many who have put country before personal safety and liberty. Vive la France!

Dr Marcel Petiot.

We print this letter without further comment. Time will be the judge of these matters.

The Arrest: October 31st, 1944

Captain Simonin of the French Forces of the Interior today arrested Captain Henri Valéry of the F.F.I. at the Métro station Saint-Mande-Tourelles.

His handwriting has matched the sample which you circulated. Beneath a heavy beard we recognized Valéry as Petiot. As Henri Valéry he has been an officer of the F.F.I. engaged in the pursuit of traitors and in our liberated motherland.

We find in Valéry/Petiot's possessions:

A variety of photographs and documents. A ration card, water-damaged on which is discerned 'Rene Kneller''' with the surname clumsily altered to 'Petiot'. The boy René, together with his parents Kurt and Margaret, disappeared after escaping by the Fly-Tox method.

It has proved impossible to reward the arresting officer Captain Simonin. He has vanished. Following detailed investigations, we now have evidence to support the belief that he was the notorious collaborator Soutif, responsible for betraying dozens of patriots to the Gestapo

November 1st, 1944 Saint-Mande-Tourelle Railway Station

Yesterday at 10.46 a.m. we apprehended the suspect on the platform before he had a chance to board. The man we now know to be Marcel Petiot wore a khaki uniform and kepi of the FFI and the armband of that force. We overpowered him, made the suspect secure and escorted him to the Reuilly Armoury. We stripped him of these raiments of disguise and ensured that he would no longer sully the honour of true Frenchmen.

Petiot had on his person: a 6.35 revolver which was loaded and which would have offered significant danger to the apprehending officers; cash to the value of over 30,000 francs; a number of forged identity papers and search and arrest warrants, no doubt to be used in his criminal misappropriation of goods.

He also carried the following identity and membership cards – Communist Party Member no. 268664 and France-USSR Friendship Committee membership no. 290974. Also, several ration cards in the names of other persons; one for a young boy called 'René'. One fears for the people named on these cards and the manner by which they were obtained.

The suspect was holding an official order under the name 'Valéry'. This was the persona under which the suspect was operating – 'Captain Henri Valéry'. The order was instructing Valéry to report for re-deployment and conveyance to the Direction Generale des Études et Recherches office in Saigon in our Indo-China territories. He was to be used as a medical officer in that country for which he was scheduled to embark on November 2nd.

It should be noted that in his possession Petiot/Valéry had a document detailing accusations against the former head of the Brigade Criminelle, Commissaire Massu, who is currently in custody and awaiting investigation. There may well be connections to be explored in that case. – Captain H. Simonin

Court de Justice de la Seine, December 1944

Pierre Bonny: I have a statement in my defence.

I wish the court to take into account my record as a policeman before the Occupation – the Lavisky case, in particular. And then a career as a respected private detective.

There was no 'Bonny-Lafont Gang'. I was compromised by the gangster Lafont and was dragged into his dark world and his dealings with the Germans.

It is true that our offices at 93, rue Lauriston were used for regrettable purposes. Lafont was an illiterate man who could not have dealt with the property and municipal details. I helped him with what was necessary with the city authorities.

I was not present when the crimes and atrocities listed in the indictment were committed. Lafont had recruited several notorious criminals whose records I knew from days as a policeman.

Gestapo Officer Hess oversaw the operations at rue Lauriston and we had no option but to obey orders.

I am not a brave man. I could have done more. There appeared to be no escape.

Judge: Really? The accused surely had 'escape' on his mind often in those dark days. He and his gang of criminals are implicated in the forthcoming trial of Dr Marcel Petiot, or Dr Eugène a near neighbour of theirs in the 16th. It is clear that one of their schemes was to supply desperate and gullible victims for the doctor's dubious escape route – 'Fly-Tox'. Bonny and Lafont were another link in the chain from Gestapo to 'escape' to disappearance and certain death. The so-called 'Bande de la rue Lauriston' was no more or less than a torture and murder organisation: the worst example of collaboration.

Bonny: I am guilty of many things, including stupidity and cowardice, but, I swear, I did not know of all the goings on at 21, rue le Sueur until March of last year and the signals of black smoke which drifted over to our building.

Fort de Montrouge, Paris,
December 26th 1944

Today we lined up against the wall and shot
Lafont, Bonny, Villaplane and their gang;
each one finished with the pistol, to make sure.
So, the heart of the French Gestapo is ripped out.

Lafont, who it is said could neither read nor write,
squealed like a piglet.
This was the man driven around the city
in his white Bentley with his moll on the front seat
beside him, Steins' and Berg's Old Masters,
gold and jewelry stuffed in the back
Our very own Capone.

The whole gang lived like kings at rue Lauriston,
number 93, where the champagne corks
popped like the eyes of the tortured Résistants in their cellar;
lobster claws cracked like ribs.
And the Germans smiled and slapped their backs.

Bonny, the shamed Police chief,
hero of the Stavisky scandal in '34
which nearly broke France and its government.
Who proved corrupt as those he pursued,
then riding on the Nazi tide, profiting from the war.

But Alexandre Villaplane, the Algerian,
stood tall at the end like the captain of our national team.
Which he had been.
Racing Club de Paris, France, the World Cup in '30,
scorer of goals: torturer, sadist, gambling crook,

fixer of horse races, chauffeur to Lafont,
craving a Bentley of his own.

The cruellest bastard of them all,
executing Résistants and Jews
for gold, furs, jewelry and cruel pleasure
along with those animals of the Légion Nord-Africaine,
the scum of our colonies brought home to fester.

Our bullets cleansed France of these stains.

But one thing remains, you know:
just a street away in the Sixteenth,
21, rue le Sueur where the body parts dissolved in lime
and the smoke from the stove drifted
to enter their windows last March –
what links these men to Dr Eugène/ Dr Petiot?

Paris, December 31st 1944

Sir,

I wish to answer the heinous charges levelled against me by that coward Roland. The publication in your newspaper of his article "Petiot – Soldier of the Reich" libels my name and insults my spirit.

The author of this letter, far from having committed dishonourable acts, far from having forgiven his torturers and even further from having aided them, adopted a new pseudonym immediately after his release by the Germans and secured a more active role in the Resistance so that he could avenge the thousands of his fellow Frenchmen killed and tortured by the Nazis. He remained in touch with his comrades and fought for the Liberation to the best of his abilities, despite the constant threat of arrest and torture and death. He is still doing all he can for the cause and begs your pardon if he cannot spare the time to get involved in the polemics on this matter. Having lost everything but his life, he is selflessly risking even that under an assumed name, scarcely hoping that pens and tongues freed at last from their shackles will now tell a truth so obvious to the unbiased, and forget the filthy Boche lies that it takes about two grains of good French common sense to see through.

PETIOT (Dr)

Taking Line Five, January 1945

This work-day morning on the Métro
at Gare du Nord
a man got on the crowded car.
One of the *Disparu* –
those returning from the camps,
forced labour, some dissidents, a rare Jew,
a steady trickle now after the flood.

And though he wore no yellow star
and there was no visible tattoo,
he wore his suffering clearly,
the blackened teeth, the sallow skin,
ill-fitting clothes and that distant stare,
the empty eyes of a Muselmann
whose vision had been worn out with horrors.

The old lady wearing entre deux guerres
Chanel tweed, jewels and a fox-fur,
rose out of her seat and offered it to him:
"Monsieur, ici." The carriage went quiet,
we all looked down at our feet,
not wishing to witness one of the walking dead.
And nothing was said. Nothing was said.

DGER Offices, Paris, February 21st 1945

We have today arrested a 'Captain Simonin' who, we can confirm, is the missing former member of the police force Henri Soutif. Soutif is wanted in connection with investigations into collaboration with the Gestapo in the Quimper region of Brittany. Soutif was zealous in his pursuit of French patriots who fought in the Resistance, many of whom were arrested, tortured, deported and executed by the Germans.

Simonin/Soutif was the arresting officer in the Petiot case and led the initial interrogation of that criminal; it may well be that evidence taken at that point of arrest may be questionable. Dr. Wetterwald/Valéry/Petiot may indeed have treated sick or wounded Frenchmen returned from the German factories and mines, but the information he claimed to have gathered may not have been passed on and shared with our American allies. He refused to name the members of his so-called Fly-Tox Resistance group, but claimed that they had targeted specifically the Gestapo office on rue des Saussaies. The accuracy and reliability of the Soutif/Petiot interrogations will certainly be compromised by this revelation of the true identity and background of the imposter and traitor Soutif. The nature of the work Valéry/Petiot/Wetterwald undertook for the Resistance cause may remain less clear than the well-documented actions of the disgraced collaborator Soutif.

February 6th, 1945: 15 avenue Mozart, 16th Arrondissement.

CODE 4 RESTRICTED ACCESS

Attention of Ambassador Jefferson Caffery, U.S. Embassy

From: Special Agents Daughters and Ayer

Sir, In response to your query.

We can report with some certainty that the matter of the suspected murderer Dr Marcel Petiot poses no immediate security risk to the US. He claims to have been with the Commies' Front National, but this may not be true.

The arrest of the suspect and charges against him are serious and have attracted much public attention and legal scrutiny. This will, no doubt, increase over the coming months.

We have referred to and collated reports, recorded interviews and agents' logs: whilst it is clear that the suspect was contacted by agents, and that he reported details of questionable events in Poland, France and other occupied territories, these points of contact have left no apparent paper trail.

We recommend that the US and its Embassy maintain a discreet silence over any issues which may arise. The French government and the lawyers involved have made no approaches as yet. We assume that while any inquiries would have to be processed in the customary manner, as France is our ally, that the Embassy would not strain to widen their field of reference. We may be invited to the ball game, but we ain't cheering for any team....

$\mathbf{\mathcal{L}ombat}$

Draft front page (photograph pending)

Doctor Petiot, whom the occupying press, for its own reasons of strategy, rendered inordinately famous, was arrested earlier this month and turned over to the Police Judiciary. In the light of many accusations of a serious and disturbing nature, his first declarations, we gather, depict him, too as a hero of the Resistance; this is to be proven.

We, at Combat, believe that we have fulfilled our obligation to France and to the truth by presenting this news without commentary. We will do the same as the case progresses, but we refuse to glorify an affair which is repugnant in so many of its aspects. Far too many tragic and urgent problems demand this nation's and this country's attention for us to permit ourselves to go into the scandalous details of such a sensational news item.

As the clouds of oppression lift and the light of liberation dawns, truths will appear and with the advancing armies of victory the abiding decency and honour of France will be re-established.

Albert Camus *Combat* Editorial

Daily Mirror

NOV 4

No. 12,756
ONE PENNY
Registered
at the G.P.O.
as
a Newspaper.

* *

NEW MEN QUIC

Accused of 50 murders

This is Dr. Marcel Petiot, the Frenchman who, say the police, is one of the most staggering men in the history of crime.

Petiot is accused of more than fifty murders in a death chamber in Paris, and was arrested while working unsuspected as an interrogating officer with the F.F.I.

Photograph shows him under arrest at police headquarters with his evening meal of a piece of bread, cheese and pint of water in a wine bottle.

Last night a captain at the F.F.I. barracks said:

CROSSING treacherous quicksands, British and Canadian assault troops yesterday made another surprise landing from the sea on Walcheren Island, last stronghold obstacle to the safe use of Antwerp as a great supply port.

They struck as Germans in other parts of Walcheren were trying to escape by sea

May hold up election to save security plans

By Your Political Correspondent

FEAR on the part of the Labour Party that the Social Security and other vital measures may not be carried through may yet mean the postponement of the General Election.

unanimous approval in the Labour Party, but I believe that when the Party conference meets in December a strong effort will be made by the leaders to prevent the passing of any resolution which would tie the party to any specific event at the moment when its

The Release of Madame Georgette Valentine Petiot (née Lablais)

The accused man's wife has again been released as there is still little in terms of concrete evidence held against her. Despite the fact that it is almost inconceivable that she could not have known or suspected the dubious and criminal nature of Petiot's activities, she was clearly shocked and in an unstable emotional state when we arrested her. There is the concern for her son who was sent to school in Auxerre and to be looked after by his uncle. The boy must needs be blameless in all these matters. When we arrested her at the station at Auxerre she claimed to be trying to return with her son.

When we accompanied her to the apartment at rue Caumartin we did discover a quantity of chocolate, coffee and sugar – black market, no doubt. As well as considerable stocks of morphine and heroin. Amongst various anatomical specimens in jars, there was a carving of a bizarre figure with an enlarged penis. Without blushing, she explained that her husband had carved this for his own amusement. We were unable to find the cache of jewelry and valuables which we had been led to believe were hidden in the apartment. "I have nothing but a string of pearls, my wedding band and this ruby ring, which were presents from my husband. He bought them fairly for me."

Asked to explain the quantities of goods and art objects that her husband often brought home, she stated, "The auction house Drouot will vouch for him as a regular bidder and customer. Marcel would indulge his collecting of the finer things. So many, I could not keep a list of such things. There were exotic prints. Well, erotic, I suppose. Men collect such things and that is not a crime."

We cannot prove that the wife was familiar with 21, rue le Sueur: Petiot had several buildings and businesses in the city, as well as the properties owned by Madame Petiot's father, a successful butcher and restaurateur. Few women would concern themselves with the workings of business as long as the couture bills were paid. She did not protest at her husband's purchase of this large, old property: "Marcel knew about these business dealings and, besides, he had plenty of money from his medical practice."

She knew nothing of the implications of that medical practice – the drugs, the abortions, the connections with the worst criminal elements in the city.

Awkward questions would often bring her to the point of fainting. Make of that what you will.

Also, we have discovered that 21, rue le Sueur, as well as several other Petiot properties are registered in the name of Gerhardt Georges Claude Félix Petiot, their sixteen-year-old son.

There is little to add to what Commissaire Massu had reported immediately after the discoveries at rue le Sueur and her initial arrest. She surely cannot be completely innocent in the Petiot affair. She may be unable to face the whole truth for herself. On the other hand, she may be up to her pretty, pearl-lined neck in it and be one of our most talented actresses.

2
The Soldier and the Doctor

Madame Petiot

She's a foxy one, alright, Georgette,
with a classy black astrakhan coat, her yellow leather suitcase,
the better side of forty, I'd say,
and when her hair and composure's in place
quite the type you'd not kick out of bed.

What she really knew is anyone's guess;
the brother was obviously up to his armpits in the affair,
carting over the quicklime, covering his tracks with clumsy lies,
but you could take it, almost take it,
that she was unaware.

Petiot is a crafty, devious, persuasive bastard,
a consummate actor who is plausible and charming.
A killer, no doubt, many times over
who fooled the police and the Germans –
though they were often happy to be led away

from what they did not want to see or deal with.
How could she keep tabs on all his comings and goings,
the various properties, his clients, confidants and patients?
That charge against her of stolen goods for the five-carat ring
he gave her was never going to stick, a husband's gift.

And when they took her to view the rue Caumartin apartment,
pushing though the crowds – it was said a thousand gawkers –
she turned on them and screamed her innocence.
Who knows? But when they took her fingerprints
nothing matched their records; she was clean.

Though, evidently, she'd had an extra finger removed from each hand, probably cut off at birth – polydactyly. So, nothing's as simple as it seems, you see.

Petiot the Poilu, 1917

After the incident at Chemin des Dames
they knocked me out for the pain and I came
to in the dressing station set up in the churchyard.
This was the cathedral at Sens.
Artillery bursts lighting up the night sky behind the steeple,
the ruins of the church jagged as if the whole of religion was
   broken.
My foot throbbed and bled – stigmata, I thought.

That poor wretch on the cross, two feet pierced,
his side, his head spiked.
I began to see how you could get through that,
and at the other side, not give a shit,
but look after number one, do whatever
it takes to press on, to squeeze life to the core.

Is that what they call "finding religion"?

Field Hospital, Craonne, 1917

After three years out here in this madness
you get to know the truth, the reality –
the ones who won't make it through the night,
the men with their guts held in by our bandages,
the bloody stumps of legs and arms, mangled hands.

And then there's the crazies, the shakers, most of 'em for real,
gone away from the world into whatever dreams
are still possible for them; and the shitters,
the con-men, the men who've bought
one-way tickets back to the Gard du Nord
and a glass of red on the boulevard.

Like this guy Petiot, machine gun corps,
with shrapnel in his left foot. Maybe.
Maybe not.

You can do it by ramming a grenade up a piece of piping
and standing on the end. Bad, pretty bad,
but not bad enough to stop you working and fucking
after this show is over,
because this year we will beat the Boche
push them back over the Aisne,
all the way back to Germany.
Three cheers for Pétain!

A glass of red with your mates in the café,
if any of them are left,
with stories to tell: "You should have seen
what we did to them at Chemin des Dames.
We gave them hell, believe me."

But that crafty bastard is complaining about the moaning
from bed four, where the kid's head's been caved in
and likely not seeing tomorrow morning.
Time for another injection, the big one.

The Faculty of Medicine,
the University of Paris

I can confirm that

PETIOT Marcel, André Felix,

is a graduate of the Medical School in Paris

December 15th, 1921.

Dr Petiot has successfully completed two years of study and practice in Dijon – anatomy, chemistry, physiology, histology, osteology, dissection (honours).

Dr Petiot successfully undertook his third and final year (under the accelerated programme for serving soldiers) at this university. Honours were awarded in respect of his dissertation. The thesis was 'A Contribution to Research work in the field of Progressive Paralysis and Nerve Degeneration: Landry's Disease'.

We have no reason to suppose that this was the work of another hand.

We commend Marcel André Felix Petiot to the medical profession of France.

Professor D.T. Claude

1923 Villeneuve-sur-Yonne

Dr. Marcel Petiot of the Faculty of Medicine, Paris, former intern at hospitals and asylums, treats patients with the most modern methods but without exploiting them. As a result, the sick that have any sense have the utmost confidence in him. Villeneuve-sur-Yonne: telephone 24.

'This town already has two established doctors who are well known to the citizens. What need have they of someone new?'

'Except he has a way about him, talks to you like an equal, offers cigarettes, even meals. It's the modern way and time for a change, I'd say. When those two old buggers give up on you, he's worth a try and gets results. Cured that Raymonde boy when all else had failed.'

'Maynaud, our fine mayor and pharmacist, has already had rows with Petiot about the doses he gives. But Maynaud, the new doctor says, waters down his stuff for profit anyway. Who knows?'

'I say, whatever works, works. Petiot may not be all that he seems, but give him a try. What's the harm?'

1927 Villeneuve-sur-Yonne, Le Bistro Denis.

'The man is a Red, I tell you, not a true Frenchman. Mayor Petiot – I spit – is a crook and a whoremonger. That housekeeper of his was as plump as a cow with calf. Housekeeper! Companion! He had his leg over every night. The only cooking she did was between her legs! Up the stick and only a matter of months in his house.'

'But he's a clever man – you have to give him that – a good doctor by all accounts. Why, he saved Gabriel's son last spring, staying up with him through the night when the boy fell sick with that fever. Never charged a sou, either.'

'Never bought a leg of lamb or a bottle of wine, after that either. Oh, yes, such he's a good doctor that does disappearing tricks with belly-fruit. Trouble is, he magics the woman away as well! That new wife of his had better look out for herself, you know.'

'That's dangerous talk, Michel. That woman – what's her name – Louisette Delaveau just got fed up and left him, I heard. And who could blame her? He's a scruffy mess at the best of times. Smells of days old clothes when he bends over to examine you. And stingy – just jacking up that old car of his when it breaks down and repairing it himself in his suit and tie. Grease and dirt. Did you see a doctor ever do that?'

'Louisette. She was a strapping piece of skirt – twenty-three, twenty-four at most, she was. And wasn't there that torso found over towards Auxerre just off the road in a field. A woman's body with no head and gutted. Things like that don't happen around here, do they?'

'Life's getting interesting round the old town. And I'm not going to cross him, that's for sure. Mine's another Pernod, when you're going.'

'And what about the church cross. He went on for months about it, our mayor did. "I shall rid our fair town of that monstrosity", he'd say to anyone who'd ask.'

'I've heard as how he phones up the gendarmerie to tell them that it's going to disappear – and then one morning the next week the town wakes to find it's gone, spirited away as an act of God. With Julien's old tractor heard on the square in the early hours, there's little mystery. And when the gendarmes accosted him, he said, "I do not believe I have the cross on my person," and shut the door on them. And they dragged the river and searched high and low. That Cross of Calvary must have ascended to heaven...'

'Well, he's a character, that's for sure, a real clever joker.'

'A great one for disappearing tricks. Doesn't get on with the Brigadier Gouraud, either. He's always trying to get one over the law, I reckon. Don't blame him for that, anyway, fucking greedy pigs, the lot of them.'

'But he's been stealing electricity from the supply wires with his dodgy connections, it's said. And litres, tanks full of fuel so that his car never runs out – the mayor's car strictly for official business, of course... Was there ever a man in office for taking the piss?'

'And the petrol.'

March 1928 – Le Bistro Denis

'Christ – what a night! Quick – a brandy, I'm fucking shivering and it's not just the cold air.'

'You look like shit. What's up, now?'

'That red sky and the commotion. The dairy's gone up in flames – Debauve's place – with her inside, they say.'

'What?'

'Half of the place gutted and the worst of it is that she's a goner – body all burned up.'

'That handsome, bonny lady. And an asset to the town, if you know what I mean. She could have kept us in milk with those big jugs, never mind the herd. Burned in the fire – what a way to go? I'd hate that.'

'Well, the word is that it wasn't the flames or the smoke that did for her. Gourand and his crew have been over there and found her with her head caved in, smashed with a hammer or something.'

'Robbers?'

'You might say so.'

'Jesus and the Holy Mother! That dairy was a money-maker for the town and there must have been a fair few burned francs in the blaze.'

'They've found some, but there's surely more missing.'

'And Debauve is definitely dead?'

'That's what our brave Gendarmes say; even that lot are not so slow as to miss a caved-in head. Gourand's strutting around in charge and they're sniffing through the debris. But, I tell you, that our mayor and coroner is nowhere to be seen. And he should be there, shouldn't he? Spotted driving off up the road to Sens, passing the dairy when the flames were still flickering and the smoke was drifting.

That Petiot – some fucking mayor, some fucking doctor.'

May 1928 – Le Bistro Denis

One more glass of Pernod Fils – it's my bar and I'll break open the real stuff – and I'll tell you the rest… Everything Frascot knows

I'm good for my age, yes, because I only drink the best stuff and I ride my bike. Every evening you'll see me take a turn up through the Sens Gate and back to the bistro. Often, I pass the Faubourg St. Nicholas dairy and Mme. Debauve's place, she lives alone and keeps the light on so I can clock what's going on and how she is. Petiot, our illustrious mayor, is often there with his battered car and his loud voice – lots of laughing – he's getting on like a house on fire – ha – with the buxom Debauve.

So, when the place went up and her in it, I told the flics, but they couldn't prove a thing. Accidents happen, don't they? A fine woman goes up and with her all the records of the dairy and the money besides, I suppose. And the hole in her skull could have been falling beams, couldn't it?

And to think that he first met her at our supper table, I introduced them. He was smitten, I tell you, and she was a lively piece with a bright tongue and he was easily smitten – a crowbar in his pants! My wife saw that.

I should talk to Gouraud a bit more; there's things I could tell him, maybe…

That one's more than a match for our Commie mayor.

June 1928 Villeneuve-sur-Yonne

OBITUARY

Our fellow citizens will be saddened to learn of the sudden death of a well-regarded business man, Monseur Henri Frascot, who for many years was the proprietor of the Bistro Rouge on the rue du Pont. He was a genial host and, in his youth, one of the best cyclists in this area. He leaves only his widow, Madame Frascot. There are no children. The cause of death was recorded by Dr Marcel Petiot as "an accident from a shock to the heart or some unknown side effect resulting from a hypodermic injection to alleviate chronic rheumatic pain".

A funeral mass will be held on Thursday the 24th at the Church of Our Lady.

A Notice of the New Saint-Lazare Clinic
Opens April, 1934

Dr Marcel Petiot, highly-qualified and regarded
practitioner in medicine and innovative cures,
announces his clinic for the benefit of fellow
citizens at 66, rue Caumartin, next to the
Printemps and Galerie Lafayette emporiums.

The doctor offers painless childbirths, radical
therapies and expert drug administration
guaranteed to address the following
conditions:- rheumatism, ulcers, neuralgia,
sciatica and cancer.

He is qualified to use X rays, infrared rays,
electrotherapy, diathermy, ionization therapy
and many of the latest techniques as a means of
curing his patients.

Certificates and endorsements available on
request.

For an appointment: call 3798 or in person.

Maison de Santé d'Ivry, 1936

Patient 5793 – M.A.H.F. Petiot

I find the patient to have recovered from what was surely a temporary affliction. Petiot presented as a classic cyclothymic, but a course of rest and hydrotherapy has returned him to an acceptable level of normal and workable behaviour. Whilst there is undoubtedly an underlying imbalance of character and psyche, this is manageable and one sees no reason why this man may not return to society and an occupation.

It may be assumed that the incident which precipitated this imbalance, namely that of being apprehended in the act of stealing a book from Joseph Gilbert's on the boulevard Saint-Michel, was an act out of character and unexplained by personal or family history or, indeed, by our subsequent treatment of the patient. His incoherence in the police station at the time of the arrest may be explained by the trauma of that experience.

We noted that his garbled excuses regarding his distraction and obsession with a perpetual motion machine and on another occasion that of inventing a pump to alleviate chronic constipation would have suggested that a serious breakdown of both intellect and rationality has occurred. This is not unheard of in the cyclothymic presentation: the subject being completely convinced of his own narrative, no matter how far-fetched it might seem.

The patient himself casts doubt on the record of his having been hospitalized with a mental disorder at the end of the war; his claims to have been attended to because of a suspected contraction of syphilis is, one has to concede, more probable at that time.

After another week of observation, we may assuredly discharge Marcel Petiot as free from delirium, hallucinations and pathological excitations, ready to return to normal society.

Dr Achille Delmas, Director of Clinic

Villeneuve-sur-Yonne, 1937

Mayor Petiot:
you are charged with malpractice in high office,
having taken fuel and electricity illegally
whilst in office.

Nonsense!

This is political and dreamt up
by my enemies who are unable to beat me in a fair election.
There can be no proof.

There is proof.

We have witnesses.

We have documents.

Traitors!

I have your names and addresses…

3
Monsieur de Paris

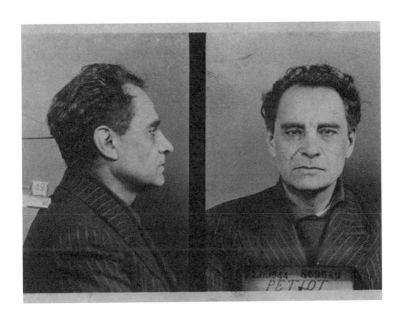

Draft Headlines, January, 1946

Petiot – the Devil's Doctor

Invalided Soldier of the Great War

Petiot – with the dark, brooding sex appeal of a movie star

Former mayor of Villeneave-sur-Yonne

Medical practitioner of that town

Petiot – the incarnation of Lucifer himself

Mastermind of the Fly-Tox Resistance Method of escape

Petiot – the poet of hell with butcher's hands

The dark doctor of the occupied city

The secret witness of slow deaths

The star of the biggest show in town

Preying on the desperate and the outcasts

Plausible play-actor of death

Delivering all to their fate with a smile on his face.

Paris: March 18th, 1946

Roll up
Roll up
Come on in
Roll up and watch the fun begin

We've had the war
We've skinned our cats
(And ate 'em, haven't we, Ma?)
We've razored pimps and quislings
We've decorated street lamps
With guilty dolls
Hoods and molls
We've shaved their head
And burned their beds

Roll up
Roll up
Come on in
Roll up and taste the sin

Roll up and see the big one
Madame Guillotine squeaks
Bluebeard's tiny chopper leaks
The blade glints in the sun
The crowd holds its breath
Then down it comes!

Roll up
Roll up
The circus of doom
Is about to resume

It's the place to be seen
Petiot squeezed in the crush
The rush – politicians
Gentlemen of the press
Doctors and morticians
Actors and musicians
What a mess

Roll up
Roll up
Come on in
Roll up and hear the din

The carved-up fiancées
Of that beast Landru
Have nothing on this one now,
Petiot's crimes are countless
So he claims –
The war's to blame
The war's to blame

He deals from the bottom of a loaded pack
The patriot card –
Resistance don't you know

Roll up, roll up
And take a look
At the doctor's book
Le Hasard Vaincu
Hot off the press
Why, he'll even sign a copy for you…

1946, March 18th, Grande Salle des Assises, Palais de Justice, Paris

'I am Mâitre Véron acting for the prosecution. Marcel Petiot, you are charged with the murder of

Francois Albertini	known as 'The Corsican'
Ludwig Arnsberg	
Ludwika Arnsberg	
Gilbert Basch	
Marie-Anne Basch	
Annette Basset	known as 'La Puce', 'The Flea'
Dr Paul Braunberger	
Jean-Marc van Bever	
Claudia Chamoux	known as 'Lulu'
Yvon Dreyfus	
Adrien Estébéteguy	known as 'Le Basque'
Josephine Aimee Grippay	known as 'Paulette la Chinoise'
Joachim Guschinov	
Denise Hotin	
Marthe Khait	
Kurt Kneller	
Margeret Kneller	
Joseph Piereschi	
Joseph Reocreau	known as 'Le Boxeur' or 'Iron Arm Joe'
Gisèle Rossmy	
Franzischa Schonker	
Maurice Wolff	
Lina Wolff	
Rachel Wolff	
An unrecognized young female	

In all, twenty-seven persons.
What do you say to this?

You must be joking!
No, I executed sixty-three persons and they were all enemies of my country –
France!

'Very well. But you must excuse us if we proceed with twenty-seven to begin with.'

Le Chien Noir bar in the
16th arrondissement

Tell me what he did, this Petiot,
This vampire of the sixteenth. Tell me.
Those so-called victims were scum,
junkies, whores, hoods – Jo le Boxeur –
who sliced up the face of my mate Pierre –
Adrien le Basque,
Paulette la Chinoise.
Lulu Chamoux
– harder-faced types you'd not have found
in the whole of Vichy:
collaborators with open arms
and ready cunts
for the Gestapo and the Milice
to rob and bump off true Frenchmen.

That crafty fox and his phoney Fly-Tox
put down some vermin –
I say fair enough!

'But those Jews just trying to get away
        – the Knellers, the Wolffs?'

Ah – but those people always have it tough.

Commissaire Lucien Pinault: Examination of Valéry/Petiot case, February 25th, 1945.

…The witness Jean Emile Fernand Duchesne of the F.F.I. testifies that Valéry had joined them in September of last year and came with the highest recommendations of Resistance work over a number of years with the 'Fly-Tox' group of patriots. It was claimed that Valéry and his group had been responsible for the disruption of many German army activities and the deaths of many soldiers. The man Valéry, who Duchesne came to realise was in fact Dr Petiot, also spoke of executing sixty-three people, all enemies of France. He had shot several himself, he claimed.

…The rooms where the suspect had lived the previous year under his alias were the property of a Belgian, Georges Redouté on rue du Faubourg Saint-Denis. They had a long-standing relationship following the treatment of Madame Redouté by Petiot in his role as medical practitioner. The Belgian testifies that Valéry/Petiot rarely went out in public during this period because he was being pursued by the Gestapo. He did speak of the bodies discovered at rue le Sueur in the March of that year as 'unfortunate'. Colleagues in his Resistance group had been unable to remove these and thus had to resort to the burning of corpses which alerted the authorities. It was during this period that Petiot grew a beard and affected dark spectacles. He passed his time with reading and playing dice-poker alone.

…Petiot explained the presence of an historic military drum in his rooms on rue du Faubourg Saint-Denis, now known to have been taken from the Place de la Republique, as booty retrieved during the liberation of the city. Petiot claimed to have been part of the Resistance forces who were active in the taking of Paris.

…It is clear that those who encountered Petiot/Valéry, though suspicious of his identity, recent history and activities, were taken in by the versions of his life and wartime work which he had practised. It is difficult to build a reliable account of the man and his role in the years of the German occupation or subsequently as 'Captain Valéry' in the F.F.I.

April, 1945, Gare de Lyon

To greet this train General de Gaulle himself was on the platform. Carriages of women released from Ravensbrück in exchange for our return of some German women left behind in France.

Sisters, mothers, women and girls all held back and anxious to see their loved ones, cheering and waving bunches of spring flowers, snapped branches of lilacs whose heady perfume cut through the smoke and steam of the locomotive. But not through the darkness of the faces that emerged. The fallen flowers were trodden across the platform and made a slimy purple carpet from which rose some memory of spring overwhelmed by the stench of what Ravensbrück had meant and what was brought home.

Those poor women's eyes were sunken and framed by the dark hollows of their brows. The journey they had been on was not ended there.

And though the dahlias and zinnias would bloom in the Tuileries that late spring and into summer, though the chestnut trees would be more magnificent than ever in the Luxembourg Gardens that autumn, and though the great general had saluted and wept there at the station, those women would move on to years of the unreal, the broken dreams, the tainted time of the survivor.

Palais de Justice, Paris / Fresnes Prison, Summer 1945.

The *Épuration Légale* was inevitable and could not come soon enough for many: lance the boil, burn the witch, cleanse la belle France, body and soul.

The calls for Marshal Pétain to be brought to justice grew louder and louder. The old soldier, the Marshal, the hero of Verdun and the collaborationist leader, had been smuggled over the border into Switzerland by his German masters. And then, strangely, the old boy insisted he be returned into France to answer his critics. He was driven across the border in a limousine at Verrières-sous-Jougne and then by Pullman carriage was taken on to Paris. General Koenig, leading the reception committee, refused to shake hands with the Marshal.

At the end of July he was tried, but both the Communists and the former Resistance were baying for blood. His only defence was cloaked in the ambiguity and confusion of the Occupation: had he been playing the long game, appeasing the Germans to further protect the majority of citizens? Wasn't the real criminal his prime minister Pierre Laval? How far removed from the realities of the day to day violence and atrocities could Pétain have been? He was doomed once it had been made clear that he had known of Klaus Barbie's reign of terror in Lyon, in particular the rounding up and deportation to their deaths of Jewish children from that city in August of 1942.

Guilty. And what saved him from the executioners? Why, General Charles de Gaulle himself: the brotherhood of the trenches. He commuted the death sentence to life in solitary confinement. And in what hell-hole did he see out his last six years, dying at the age of ninety-six? The Île d'Yeu in the Atlantic off the coast where Rigaud and Dufy painted and where the poet Guégan polished his gem-like haiku. And did the old warrior have a copy of *Mystique des Tempêtes* in his library there?

> Now Atlantic storms
> block out the light that might save
> an old man drowning.

At the beginning of August Pierre Laval stood trial. At first, he protested to his three lawyers that he would be exonerated; when it quickly became clear that the court and its jury were toxic, he withdrew his presence from that court and his defence collapsed.

On the establishment of the Vichy regime, Pétain had proclaimed, "Monsieur Laval and I walk hand in hand." But in court Laval, the most powerful and notorious collaborator, had cut a pathetic figure, wearing a crumpled suit, a battered Homburg and a grubby white tie, like a gangster on the run. He had presented as a beaten man, in need of sympathy. There was none, as the jury was packed with Resistance men and those he would have sent to the camps.

Guilty.

Laval, it seems, was dragged half-conscious from his cell to face the firing squad. The riflemen were mostly drunk – a common practice. He had tried to finish himself off, but the cyanide he'd hidden about his person must have been spoiled or old and served only to rack him with pains short of his release from this world. They held him down and stilled his convulsions to pump the stuff out of his stomach. It must have worked partially because he was lifted to his feet and strapped to a chair by which means they dragged him out into the courtyard to his end. He wore no shoes and had soiled himself. And this was the most powerful man in France, probably more powerful than the old Marshal, and therefore, it was argued, more guilty.

The other inmates at Fresnes Prison went wild as the shots echoed around the place: bars and doors hammered and feet stamping. They shouted, 'Bastards! Crooks! Assassins!' Laval still had his supporters at the end. Or perhaps the others knew that they'd likely face the same fate.

Central Organisation for Deported Jews

American Joint Distribution Committee of New York

Missing Persons Request

February 24th, 1945

Name: Kurt Kneller

Age: 37(?)
Country of birth/origin: Germany
Spouse: Margeret (née Lent) b. France. Age 35 (?)
Child/Children: René (male – 7 years)
Last known place/person contact: Paris, France, December 1942.
Last contact – Mlle. Roart, 6, avenue du Général-Balfourier.
Other Information: France Foreign Legion, 1939-1940; trade – electrician.
Report of postcards received with postmarks Paris and Castres.

Missing ( )

Unknown ( )

Deceased ( )

Please reply: S.O.D.P. - 503, 47th Street, New York, USA

Letter to D.S.O.D.P. New York City USA

August 21st, 1945
M. Gollety
Juge d'Instruction
The Case of Marcel Petiot

It is my task to inform you that in response to your missing persons enquiry form of February 24th it must be said that we are proceeding with an investigation and court trial of one Dr Marcel Petiot for multiple murders committed in this city over several years. While it is not certain at this point that the missing persons whom you seek – the Knellers, Kurt, Margeret and their son René – are among those thought to have been murdered by the accused, their disappearance to which you refer would seem to suggest that there may well be cause for concern.

There is evidence even at this stage to point towards their involvement with the accused in a very suspect escape network during the German occupation of Paris. Items found at the scene of Petiot's crimes, together with witness statements which we are in process of collating, give one little hope that the Knellers were not victims of this man's criminal network.

I shall undertake to have my office appraised of your concern and will ensure that they inform you of developments. We should be ready to go to trial later this year, though I must stress that there are a number of potential victims and a great deal of evidence to process.

M Goletty

Café Bézarie March, 1946

Monsieur? You want a ticket for the show, mon ami?

What show?

The murderer Petiot, of course.

Ah, he's guilty. A Communist, a cheap card-carrier and traitor.

Guilty? Well, the whole world and his cousin knows that. But the maggot squirms well on his hook and that circus parade of witnesses is the best show in town. Beats 'The Mad Woman of Chaillot' – and it's real!

Who wants to see a bunch of crooks and pimps and professors go through the motions? I have had enough of them on our street, all over the 16th.

Listen, do you know how hard these tickets are to get hold of? All sorts of high class and stars are going to the proceedings, like an opening night – Paulette Dubost (remember her in 'The Rules of the Game'?), Marcel Pagnol and Josette Day 'La Belle et la Bête' eh – how right is that? – the cream of the city – Chevalier, Picasso, you name 'em… Playboys, big spenders, even the Duke of Monaco – Rainier – they're all there.

Chevalier! That collaborator goes to see what should happen to the likes of him. A songbird for the Nazis.

What's the rush, anyway? It will be on for weeks more – all those murders. And the long-winded lawyers dragging it out for the francs.

Listen. Two weeks, maybe three. They're not going to waste too long on a guy as bang to rights as that Petiot. But, I tell you, what a character: he's signing copies of his book, hot off the press, *Le Hasard Vaincu*, the thing he wrote in prison. He's like a fucking film star signing for fans. Hundreds of them, even the Judge Leser has his copy signed! Petiot's some shit, but you have to admire the guy's cheek. He's there telling Véron about the Resistance, about using 'le plastique', how to set and detonate explosive charges, tying them to Bosch stick grenades and throwing them at Germans in the Bois de Boulogne. Though no-one saw the corpses. Trying it in with Véron, who was himself a Major in the Maquis, a real hero!

What about Floriot, that slick bastard of a prosecutor, they're writing about?
See, you *are* interested: he's a cool operator. A fighter. Sweet Mother, has he got some characters out of the shit! Some Boches and some quislings too.

With them it's a job: the client pays and those smooth bastards wax eloquent.
But Petiot, the mad Doctor Death, has a few tricks himself. Listen: Véron has just scored a point – really witty – and Petiot compliments him. He says, "Monsieur, I should recommend my clients to you." And Véron comes back quick as a whip: "It would be safer for you to send me clients than for me to send some to you." That brought the house down.

Come on. This guy's been doing his dirty stuff all over the 16th: he could be your neighbour.

Two tickets – Ok, how much?

Palais de Justice: The Facts

Petiot: ...and furthermore, the court should take into account my efforts over a number of years to resist the Nazi occupiers of our fair France. Has no-one mentioned my work in Lyon when our group was instrumental in rescuing the British agent whose drop had been spotted by the enemy and who would surely have been tortured for vital information by the Gestapo? The four hundred or so local prostitutes we mobilized to...

Judge Leser: Enough! Silence the witness. We have had too much of this far-fetched nonsense – secret weapons used silently and invisibly against the Germans in the Bois de Boulogne, an army of prostitutes deployed by the enemy in Lyon, strategic war secrets passed on to our allies. There is no proof in support of such claims. We direct the accused to address those questions put to him regarding the fate of Yvan Dreyfus, as directed by his family's counsel.

Mâitre Véron: Thank you, your honour. Now what do you say to explain the disappearance and probable murder of Monsieur Dreyfus? His family and the court have a right to know.

Petiot: Dreyfus? What do you care about Dreyfus – Jews and traitors disappear – who cares? Dreyfus was a stooge in the pay of the Gestapo, a traitor to his country, his religion and his race. The Germans planted him to bring down our Fly-Tox organization.

Mâitre Véron: These are foul and heinous accusations to cover the tracks of a self-confessed murderer, a bestial, unfeeling being who betrayed his country and his profession.

Petiot: Shut up! What do you know of the real fight, the Resistance and what we did to save France. The execution of traitors and collaborators was necessary – and could be brought into play again if those baying animals in the public gallery – yes you – don't heed their actions. I'll have names, I warn you! And you weaselly counsells for the scheming and lying prosecution. You lot were baying for a different Dreyfus not so long ago and look where that got you. And him. Jews matter when it suits you.

Mâitre Véron: And what suits you, Petiot? Any person of whatever race, religion or family who can be duped into bringing you their possessions in the hope of escaping their fate. And you bring them a fate that they could not have dreamt of.

Petiot: These are your dreams and have nothing to do with the facts.

Mâitre Véron: Ah, yes, the facts. We shall introduce you to the facts as this trial uncovers them.

Palais de Justice: Outstanding Patriotism

Maître Véron: After the discovery of the crimes you had perpetrated at rue le Sueur you disappeared, didn't you?

Petiot: I had my Fly-Tox men to protect against the Germans. The less everyone knew, the better. So we could continue our fight for France.

Maître Véron: Ah, yes, your outstanding patriotism and your ingenious schemes to liberate your country and, at the same time to liberate countless valuables and possessions from those poor people who trusted in you and believed in your fantastical escape network.

And then Doctor Marcel Petiot disappears and two other men are born – Dr Wetterald and Captain Valéry. Two miraculous births – that's a bit much even for a man of your exceptional talents, Petiot.

Petiot: In those difficult days it was commonplace for those fighting for liberation to switch names and identities. Anyone engaged in our struggles would know that.

Maître Véron: I see. But those two versions of yourself continued long after the liberation of this city, long after the fate of France was assured. And who knows how much longer into your sordid life these noms de guerre might have proved necessary for your escape from justice?

Petiot: I continued to work for my country and served with distinction in the F.F.I. when that opportunity presented itself. I would still be working for France if these pointless proceedings had not interrupted my life. There is still work to be done.

Maître Véron: And working for France entailed the amassing of a substantial cache of valuables – jewelry, even a fine stamp collection – First and Second Republic rarities – which you stole and which then mysteriously disappeared from the safe at headquarters in the Reuilly Armoury. More murders and thefts. You must have written a lot of letters.

Petiot: I know nothing of these matters.

Maître Véron: I see. So, you would have us believe that you left behind your practice in Paris, your wife and child, your patients and friends to pursue selflessly your dedication to your country and cause. The Communist Party and the Tricolour.

Petiot: I realise that it must be difficult for those who did not fight, who hedged their bets and kept their heads down, difficult, I say, for those not in the front line, to understand the sacrifices others made.

Maître Véron: Oh, we shall try, Doctor Petiot, we shall try. We shall try, for example, to understand why an officer of the F.F.I. committed to re-building his country, to purifying the ills of the war, should then volunteer to be posted to the other side of the world, leaving all that behind. Of course, conveniently leaving behind all the mess he had created, the crimes he has committed.

Petiot: Rubbish! I felt that my experience and professional practice could make a real contribution to our territories in Indo-China. Some of us have a sense of national service and honour.

Maître Véron: I see. And your application for this posting was supported by colleagues – you were recommended by no less a person than F.F.I. officer Doctor Wetterwald. A man who knew you better than anyone, Petiot – for, as we have seen Wetterwald was also Petiot. And also Valéry. High praise indeed!

At the Club de Croc

Ladies and gentlemen, boys and girls, officers and other ranks...
and those two blokes in the corner wearing Homburgs making
notes... welcome to the Club Croc where the fun is for all, the
song never ends and the booing never begins... not until tonight,
you say...

Everyone got their glasses full, eh? More foie gras, my lovely? You
don't have to ration yourself, if you get my meaning, the back
door of Croc's is always open.

Here. Have you heard the one about the Paris doctor, oh, oh, for
Petiot, with a cure for everything – cancer, in-growing toenails,
piles, nerves, babies wot shouldn't have been there?

No? Well, he must be good because none of his patients ever
complained – cos no-one has seen them since... Boom. Boom...
Perhaps we should book him in here as *The Great Petiot!*

His consulting room is the smallest you've ever seen and the last
one those patients would ever see. 'Oh, dear Doctor, why must I
wear these chains and stand against that wall?'

'Don't worry, those chains have magic powers and will transport
you to your dreams. And let me give you this little injection –
madame, no little prick has bothered you before, has he? I promise,
you will feel, nothing,' (as her husband and his friends used to say).

'You are too hot in those furs? Let me help you off with that fox
or bear or rabbit or beaver – your Maison Coco Chanel must
have raided the city zoo for that outfit. You'll be hot enough
where you're going, believe me.'

Hey, this beauty here tonight at the front table: you'd not mind a bit of chains and whips by the look of you. A woman of the world, I'd say.

And who were these patients of the good doctor, you ask. Well, the highest of the best of high society – Adrien le Basque, Jo le Boxeur, Lulu and the Corsican, the Bedbug and La Chinoise – all perfect dinner party guests, though you'd have to hide the best silverware. And they'd bring their own knives.

You know, the sort of people you'd have round for dinner, the sort of people you'd happily lend a few francs to (if you wanted to keep both your ears for a while longer).

'Need some lime in your gin? I've got plenty of that in my cellar and canapés and fresh meat you can pick the bones of,' says Doctor Petiot.

Hey, those two fedoras at the back have left. Probably noting down and stealing my best jokes.

Here: what do you say to a bloke in a dark suit walking down the Champs-Elysees?

Heil Hitler.

What do you say to a man in an officer's uniform walking on the banks of the Seine?

Heil Hitler.

What do you say to a Kapitanleutnant Kriegsmarine on the dockside in Marseilles?

Hello Sailor!

Thank you. Thank you. Especially you, madame – you've said 'allo to a few sailors, I bet.

And now for your delectation – the girl who puts the dick into delectation – your very own – the songbird of Montmartre, the Mistress of the Marais, the Princess of the Pigalle – put your specs on sir, if you haven't left them in the One-Two-Two Club, you won't recognise her with her clothes on – it's Gisèle!

Palais de Justice: Fly-Tox

Mâitre Véron: Why did you buy 21, rue le Sueur – an impressive, large house in the Sixteenth – a fine area? How did you manage to acquire such a place – formerly the home of the famous actress Cecile Sorel, I believe?

Petiot: The house suited my medical practice. It was convenient for clientele.

Mâitre Véron: A practice increased by the distribution of cheapjack brochures advertising your patent cures for everything from the pox to cancer!

This house had a sink in the basement. Was it 'convenient' that this should drain directly into the Seine?

And the 'convenient' triangular room you constructed – the cell, the gas chamber with the spy-hole that allowed you...

Petiot: That is rubbish! Tales made up to sell newspapers. This was a room planned for my X-ray machine. The holes were for electric wires, not for the 'gas' of the journalists! Their 'false button' was simply an old and disused one I had not got round to replacing. The false door was left in place in order to absorb dampness, to control humidity to facilitate the efficacy of the process. There was no viewing of 'the death throes' – what imagination the gutter press has! It was simply for me to monitor my patients during the X-ray procedure.

Mâitre Véron: How convenient.

And so, Docteur Petiot, what about the bodies, the heads, torsos, thighs, hands, hair, kilos of bones by the sack full?

Petiot: I know nothing of this; I was as shocked as anyone to discover such untidiness. I can only surmise that members of my Fly-Tox Resistance group had taken it upon themselves to use the lime-pit and stove without permission. I gave no such orders.

Maître Véron: Ah, yes, the 'Fly-Tox' group – that mysterious branch of the Resistance whose members you still refuse to name – so secret that it went unacknowledged, unrewarded, unknown to any other section of the Resistance in the whole of France. Quite a security feat! Quite an organization!

Petiot: My men know who they are. They know the honour and loyalty which they gave to France.

Maître Véron: And let us not forget your secret weapon.

Petiot: Yes, an ingenious device. We killed two German motor-cyclists in Marly Forest – at a distance of hundreds of metres. Also, Germans in the Bois de Boulogne. For France, we harvested those ripe haricots verts.

Maître Véron: And how was this achieved, by what means?

Petiot: I refuse to reveal in open court secrets which continue to be of value to France. I am prepared to share them with our army officers when the time is right.

Maître Véron: And your associates? Who were these men? Produce one of them as a witness.

Petiot: Do you think that I would drag them into all this business? They were, they are, heroes – France owes them a debt. They should be awarded the Liberation Cross for their bravery!

Mâitre Véron: Docteur Petiot, if you bring them before us, I'll guarantee them the cross, one each side of yours! Their own Calvary!

Cross-Examining for the Defence

Floriot: Doctor Petiot, is it not the case that many of the so-called victims of your Resistance group were hardened criminals and collaborators?

Petiot: Well, they certainly were. Jo le Boxeur was a monster in the pay of the Gestapo, a murderer and a torturer for the Boche. His charnel house was at rue Lauriston and many other places across the city. When we caught him he pulled a knife on us and his woman tried to tear at us with her nails. But not for long. We had him crying like a baby before the end.

And Adrien le Basque was a low-life thug polluting the clean air of Paris with his drugs and whores and the like. There were some innocents we helped to their freedom, but others were best dealt with swiftly in order to keep the escape network going.

We did the job of both the Gendarmerie and the sewer men that night. The enemies of France deserved no better than rats, be they men or molls.

Floriot: And you took no pleasure in these acts, not personal nor ambition was involved in the no-doubt distasteful side of the patriotic work you undertook.

Petiot: In 1917 I fought to the best of my ability at Chemin des Dames in the service of my country. That work to defend us against the Boche and their lackeys simply continued in my mind, as it would for any true Frenchman. A true Frenchman answers the call to arms.

Floriot: So our country owes a debt of gratitude to those who worked for the cause of freedom and liberty in a clandestine and unheralded way?

Petiot: I and my Fly-Tox brothers in arms would not have presumed to have claim to the Croix de Guerre. Though if the General and his government deem it now to be an appropriate honour, then they certainly know where to find me.

Report on Dr Marcel Petiot, 1945

He presents as the classic schizophrenic:
charming and urbane,
but with the occasional gaze of a fanatic.
You would happily take a drink with this fellow,
but be wary of walking home with him.

As a child, we have discovered, he was noted
to be somewhat isolated. He could be cruel to animals –
it is recalled that he captured and tortured small birds
taken in their garden; he caged then blinded them.

He was sufficiently proficient in his medical studies
after the war, but his war service and experiences
at the Front may well have left him with residual stresses
and anxieties. We see this in many veterans.
This, however, should not excuse behaviour
of the bestial type with which Petiot is accused.

Palais de Justice: The Knellers

Mâitre Véron: Recreux and Estébéteguy had Gestapo connections perhaps, but their women? Basset and Chamoux, Lulu and Annette, Pauleen la Chinoise, the Little Bedbug – ladies of the night, no doubt, but since when has that been a capital punishment in France, Ladies and Gentlemen?

Petiot: Whores, collaborators. Boche trash! What would you have me do with these, spare them? Would you hand them the Croix de Guerre? Collabo trash!

Mâitre Véron: And the Jews – the Wolffs, the Arnsbergs, the Basches – displaced, persecuted innocents you lured in to your fly trap and dispatched to a hotter place than Argentina!

Petiot: They were Germans, fakes! Agents turned by the Nazis. Gestapo stooges passed on to us by that bitch Eriane Kahan. I knew her for what she was. If Eriane Kahan had sent me a hundred Jews or a hundred gentiles I would have eliminated every one of those people and then that traitorous whore Kahan would have been the next in line! This is a war we were fighting.

Mâitre Véron: But the man Keller – Kurt Kneller – was a patriot, enlisting in the Foreign Legion.

Petiot: Yes, I remember the Kellers. I had treated him as a patient. Later he came to me with a wife and child, they needed to escape, to disappear quickly, but he had no money. I fixed them up through Fly-Tox – false papers and tickets to Orléans. I took their furniture against payment, though that was an act of generosity on my part, it was not the best.

After a couple of months the wife sent me a postcard to say that they were safe, but that her husband was still ill.

Maître Véron: And the son, René – seven years old?

Petiot: He went too. They took the boy, of course.

Maître Véron: Yet his pyjamas were found in the pile of clothes at 21, rue le Sueur: his name on a stitched label on the jacket.

Petiot: How should I know? I cannot keep track of all those I helped or dealt with. Maybe they were left because he'd soiled them? Why should I keep such things? Why do you think I would kill the kid?

Maître Véron: Why should we think that you didn't?

Cell 7: a child visits

Mein herr?
Monsieur? Monsieur le Docteur?
It is René.
My mother and father, where are they?
Where have they gone?

There was a dream I dreamt –
we were at your house, that big house,
we met you and you invited us in.
The night was cold and we had travelled so far.

And then a fire started and I ran from the house
through the streets… I passed
a butcher's shop, some cafés, a fountain.
The butcher's shop had carcasses of lambs hanging,
and chickens by the neck.

I stood in a doorway
when the Germans marched past.
Some of the German soldiers had flowers round their necks.
There were flowers everywhere
and they threw flowers back at the crowd.
They were kind and kissed the girls who waved.
They shook some men by the hand.

Is the war finished?
My father, my mother, where are they?

Palais de Justice : Science

Floriot: Monsieur, you say that you are an expert in these matters?

Forensic Witness: Doctor, I am a Doctor and yes, I am often called to give expert evidence on such occasions.

Floriot: And all this hair – was any of it white?

FW: No, I grant you that, there was no evidence of such hair. The number of bodies was about equally split between men and women. A child or two.

There was positively no trauma – fractured skulls, knife or bullet wounds, broken bones caused by assault. No poisons were evident. These were dissections, performed by an expert, a trained physician.

Floriot: But my client, Dr Petiot had absolutely no special instructions in the art of dissection as a medical student. There is no record of that.

FW: I am amazed. He performed a superb job of dissection at rue le Sueur without instruction then.

Floriot: I beg your pardon, Docteur, you mean that the dissector, the true perpetrator of these crimes – accomplished that.

FW: Ah, yes.

Now, as to his background: he was discharged from the army in… er… July… July 4th 1919 – a victim of neurasthenia, amnesia, mental instability, sleep-walking, suicidal depression and paranoia.

How he qualified as doctor, I can't understand, His studies were unremarkable, as far as we can tell. Though his thesis mark was 'superior'. But it is quite likely that Petiot was not the author of that, it may have been another's hand. It was a simple matter to buy such things. Dissection would have been a standard part of such studies and training, and would not have necessarily been noted. Following the war training was accelerated.

Floriot: Well, I defer to your knowledge of that probability; when and where did you train, sir?

Never mind. And my client is, in your expert opinion, sane?

FW: He is indeed.

Floriot: Yet when as Mayor of Villeneuve he was tried for the trifling misappropriation of gasoline and other related minor misdemeanors, you, sir, and your board of experts found Dr Petiot to be disturbed and not responsible for his actions.

FW: Well...

Floriot: Furthermore, how has the behavior of Dr Petiot's sister on these occasions struck you?

FW: His sister has exhibited no sign of mental disturbance.

Floriot: I am relieved to hear that, you see, Dr Petiot has no sister.

Cell 7, the author

'For France against Fascism'.
I like this title:
'For France against Fascism'.

At Fresnes they beat me,
At the Department of Jewish Affairs
they beat me but
at the German Army Centre
on the Avenue Henri-Martin
they gave me the works.

I lost three millimetres filed
from my teeth.
My head they bound in iron
to crush their truth from me.

But the worst was the water –
freezing water, my head
held under the tub until
my eyes bulged like a fish's,
my lungs bursting,
burned hollow under the freezing water.

I told them nothing. I laughed.
I confessed only
my disdain for them.
Because, I, Petiot, knew them,
knew their evil better than they did themselves.
I knew everything about the world
they were exploring. I knew
how their bodies felt

as they did those things to me.
How it was all made more real,
but distanced, as if behind glass.

They showed me a dead man
I did not know.
Another lying, writhing on a stretcher,
I did not know,
his face beaten to a pulp,
his breathing blood-bubbling in snores.

But nothing they could do,
nothing they could show me,
impressed me.
They played my game, but did not know it.

I had knowledge, conviction,
as their Hitler had conviction –
that little failed painter
who talked above his weight,
drew down forces stronger than himself.

And so, Dr Eugène, Captain Valéry,
all the Petiots contained within me,
had their measure
and I beat them at Henri-Martin,
at the rue des Saussaires
and at Fresnes I beat them
at their own games.

Le Hasard Vaincu

By Dr Marcel Petiot, published 1945.

And is not Chance the whore
of circumstance, the cog of history,
the machine that balances our lives
then minces us whole?

God and Satan are the great card players
in a game run by eternal laws so that man
is no more than a speck on the back of a card.
Ask Pétain. Ask the Marshall.
Heroes and villains.

And so it would have been down to eternity
that rough, dark tunnel of our history
had not Satan when he was Lucifer
discovered the bottom of the deck,
the thumb on the scales,
the light in the eyes,
the shade under the table,
the ace behind the yawn.

And this was according to infernal rules,
for was it not God who marked the deck
of men's souls, branding diamond
and spade and heart and club,
false colours decreed,
false colours attributed?

They brought me a priest:
he said, 'I can introduce you to God.'

I said, 'We've already met and I didn't take to him.'

In our world
let there be distinctions and rules
until they need to be broken as irrelevant.
Life is a battle only if you fight fate
(As the actress said as the curtain dropped
And as I shall proclaim as my own sharp curtain falls).

But that is another story.
I, Dr. Marcel Petiot,
doctor, thinker, author, patriot,
have worked and fought to
learn these truths for you,
too late, perhaps for this broken country.
I am your witness.

Signed

Dr. Eugène
Captain Valéry

Leader of the Resistance Group FLY-TOX

(Cell7/Sector7/Prison de la Santé – known as 'Death Row')

Petiot remembering Paris in 1940

Even in July that time in the water would have killed them
if the shelling had not.
Two thousand of our sailors killed, all ships sunk off
Mers-el-Kébir by ships of the British Navy
because de Gaulle, or the Communists or other agents
put it about that our fleet was going to be signed over to the Nazis.
Which I knew from my sources was not true.

But who listened?
Who had the sense to follow Petiot, a truthful source,
as I kept my ears to the ground and passed it on
to the Americans at Le Cinquième Bureau:
gems before swine, I tell you.
Who wanted to know such inconvenient truths?
Allies massacring allies, and not for the first time.

A man I treated, a Pole, with his dying words
told me of the slaughter at Katyn forest he had seen,
when Major General Smorawiński was killed
and eighteen thousand of his officers, each standing
on the edge of the pit, shot in the back of the head
and tipped into oblivion.
The soil bull-dozed over them all and the trees re-planted.

My enemy's enemy is my friend, of course,
even when in mid-stream he changes his horse.
The Nazis that will hang at Nuremburg
are charged with much, but Katyn was not their crime,
Stalin's NKVD had that dirt on their hands, those dead
men in their memories. Sun through the pines,
morning mist, the smells of Spring as the bullet entered the head.

Cell 7: a marital visit

Marcel.

Marcel, it's Georgette.

I am sorry. You know why it is impossible for me to come and visit you. And I cannot come to the trial. Someone has to take care of Gérard in Joigny; and there is unfinished business, as we both know.

I have been through the hands of the police, twice, and have survived, though it has taken it out of me. There are only so many times that one can faint.

The body we buried last year at the 'funeral' of your cousin Céline has been resurrected, though by whom it is not clear — your Comrades in the Party or those dark friends of yours from rue Lauriston? Whatever. I saw nothing of it, the coffin was empty when the police dug it up. The walls in rue des Lombards are now hollow. So, I have enough money and jewelry and our son will be schooled and well looked after.

I have plans to change our family name and move on from Joigny when the fuss has died down. We had talked of Lisbon, Argentina, well, if it is possible, and if you escape this mess, then we will make contact somehow.

Marcel, we both know that will not happen — they have you on the block. The Fates. And I must move on with Gérard and what remains of our lives. There are business matters too. I do not know everything you did. I did not ask. I do not wish to know.

This vision of me that you conjure up — you have my shape. But do you hear my voice? Do you hear how it has changed? I am changing. And moving on.

I shall not visit you again. I shall not haunt you.

You are on your own, Marcel.

But you were always on your own, weren't you?

Palais de Justice: Patriots

Floriot: The court has heard from various witnesses from the community of Villeneuve-sur-Yonne. All these upstanding citizens have testified to the respect paid to their mayor and coroner Dr Marcel Petiot in his time in that town. The municipal duties he performed with diligence and honesty. Occasions following the German occupation when he returned to provide the necessary papers forged for townspeople to escape persecution, not to mention the two British officers shot down and taking refuge in that area.

Now I wish to call on Lieutenant Richard L'héritier, distinguished member of the Parachute Corps who, following his capture by the Germans was imprisoned and tortured for months in the jail in Fresnes. In the summer of 1942, he shared a cell with Dr Petiot.

The court will appreciate that in these barely imaginable circumstances prisoners whose lives are bound together in a struggle to survive will become as brothers and will keep no secrets from each other.

Lieutenant L'héritier, did the accused at any point mention any of the names of the victims he is alleged to have killed?

L'héritier: He did not. But he did talk about his work for the Resistance, specifically the Fly-Tox group which he led and which was successfully enabling a number of fugitives to escape from the Nazis.

While at Fresnes he gained the respect of other prisoners by his proud rebuttals of the German guards. He gave me advice on how to out-fox their interrogation techniques; he organised a scheme to smuggle out messages from prisoners. He provided me with a number of contacts and addresses of Resistance men who would aid me if and when I were released.

Floriot: And were you able to verify and use these contacts?

L'héritier: I was not; you see, the only escape for me from Fresnes was to be sent on to the stalag.

Floriot: Were you surprised to learn that the Germans had released Petiot? Were any suspicions raised by that, as the prosecution has implied?

L'héritier: It would have been explained by the fact that he had not given up any information of worth and so they let him out and no doubt had him followed in order to learn more of his activities and associates.

When you share a prison cell with a man you learn of his true nature. Petiot was a patriot. He would never have worked for the Gestapo.

Floriot: Indeed, a patriot. But here he is in court accused of the most heinous acts, branded as an enemy of France, his actions during the Occupation called into question with many unable or unwilling to defend this patriot. What do you say to that sad state of affairs, Lieutenant?

L'héritier: I am surprised: I do not believe that Dr Petiot could have acted alone. I can only presume that he finds himself abandoned and in this position because of politics. His party, the Communists, are so desperate to grasp power that they must see him and this case as an embarrassment which they wish to avoid. They have washed their hands of their Comrade.

Petiot: Lieutenant L'héritier, dear comrade in arms, fellow resister, could any reasonable man believe that I am guilty of collaboration with the enemy we both so heartily despise?

L'héritier: I do not understand that. You are, for me, a patriot, a fellow fighter for France. I will always be proud to say that I shared a cell with you in our darkest hours.

Palais de Justice: Nézondet

Judge Leser: You are René-Gustave Nézondet, are you not?

Your name has come up at several points in these proceedings.

What have you to tell us about the accused?

Nézondet: Sir, I have known Marcel Petiot since our days together in Villeneuve-sur-Yonne, when he was our mayor. And a very good mayor too.

I was arrested by the Boche at the same time back in '44. I was sent to Fresnes and treated roughly. They wanted me to tell them about Marcel and the crimes, but I said nothing. Because I knew nothing. 'Keep me here forever, if you choose, I cannot tell you what I do not know.'

After a while they believed me. Before they let me out I asked the Doctor what it was all about and he said that he had been smuggling people out of France. And that they were going to shoot him for that. He told me to go back to his wife and tell her to go to their secret place and dig up the stuff. He said she would know what 'the stuff' was. And tell her how much he loved her.

Judge Leser: And what on did you think this 'stuff' was?

Nézondet: Sir, I did not know and I did not ask. In these times I thought it must be family money or documents, or Resistance things. All sorts of people buried all sorts of things when the Boche came.

Judge Leser: Yes. Including bodies. People killed for gain. Why do you think we are here?

Nézondet: It was later that I met his brother Maurice Petiot and he told me that, "There's enough in there to get us all shot," at rue le Sueur. He had found suitcases, false letters, syringes and poison. And there were the bodies. Maurice looked as white as a ghost. I said that Marcel must be a monster to do such things, but Maurice said, "No, he is a very sick man. We need to take care of him now." And I thought, but he's a doctor, so why should we have to look after him?

Judge Leser: Yes, the brother has appeared before us, despite his advanced sickness and feeble state. He claims that you are unreliable because you suffered at the hands of the Gestapo and that your memory is damaged.

Nézondet: Yes, I suffered, but I cannot forget the look on Maurice's face that day. And the stench of the place, 21, rue le Sueur, still on him. And the shock of learning what his brother had done.

Floriot: Your honour! The witness is not in a position to…

Judge Leser: This witness will be heard. We have precious few witnesses to what occurred at 21, rue le Sueur. The accused has made sure of that.

Café Marais, 1946

Monsieur, your health.
Ma'mselle….

The Petiot case?
Oh, yes, I am involved, you might say.
What? Lawyers? Lawyers?
I've brought them to tears – of anger
and satisfaction, when that is what they have schemed for.

After the police, the judge and the talkers,
the jury and the priests,
it is I, to me alone,
that doomed bastard comes to at last.

I am Monsieur de Paris.

And do not imagine it is a job like any other.
The last one – that killer Weidman –
was crooked on the table and his neck
missed the lunette's drop. My men
had to put the sod back into place.
And when the second time he rolled clean,
head like a football,
women from the crowd rushed to dip their scarfs
in the blood. Superstitious bitches.
Because what is it but meat?

Ma'mselle, your good health – though you look pale.

Fear not for the devil doctor –
he will meet with me tomorrow in a closed courtyard,

no more rabble, no prying eyes,
his departure from the filth of this world
is my job.
Mine the blade, mine the basket.
This hand
on this glass,
which I will happily shake with yours, monsieur,
will lift the head and sign the declaration.

Ah, you flinch, young lady –
It is but a hand like any other.
It is the hand I wipe all our arses with.

Cell 7: Lulu

Ok, it is Claudia,
Claudia Chamoux.
But call me Lulu,
everyone called me Lulu
since that pig Jo le Boxeur
ran me.

Oh, Monsieur le Docteur,
with me you made your greatest mistake –
I have had men scream with pleasure.

Monsieur, what is your pleasure?

You could have saved me, kept me,
we could have had an arrangement.
I cared nothing for that bastard Jo
and his pimp cronies, the junkies, the other whores.

I should have guessed your game
when you turned me aside and got on business-like
with the injection.
All that bullshit about escaping
after Jo conned the Gestapo
and had to run out of the city like a rat.
Which he was – a scared rat.

You have eyes like a hawk looking down
on all of us – a hawk or a wolf –
I should have seen you for what you are,
even if Jo was conned. The con-artist conned…

Why did you do all those things?
Even in the shit-hole that this city had become
you were some piece of work;
my body quartered
your hand unfeeling
on my dead, warm flesh.

Fool! Didn't you know
the dead stick to you.
You may wash us off your hands,
but we are inside you.

These nights I come to your cell,
pushing my way through
the long queue of the others –
the smell of my perfume
in your nose, a stiffening
ache in your soft prick.

Petiot – look up at me –
I spit on you!

Palais de Justice: Kahan

Mâitre Véron: You are Eryane Kahan and your involvement in the crimes of…

Petiot: Alleged crimes.

Mâitre Véron: …in the crimes of this man have been mentioned by many others. What have you to say?

Kahan: Sirs. What I tell is the truth, I swear. What I know is only that the Wolffs were desperate to escape from their fate. And this is what they had to do. I helped people. It was difficult times for all, I think. But the Wolffs and the others were not Gestapo. They were not collaborators. For sure. They were otherwise going to their deaths with the Germans and were very happy to have the promise of Dr Petiot. Which I know he gives to them.

I wanted to go with them and to use the escape he was offering. Thank goodness, I thought.

I think now that he did not want me to go. I was useful to him in his tricks.

Mâitre Véron: And Madame Kahan, it has been suggested that your disappearance following the discovery of the bodies and the crimes at 21, rue le Sueur was suspicious. Why was that? Did you realise that Petiot was a murderer?

Kahan: This is not the truth. I tell you, I was believing in the doctor and held him in – how you say – fine regards. Until I was shown the newspapers and the stories about him, afterwards. I did not know what a bad man he was, really. I could not believe these things. But I am a Jew and had to carry on in hiding. For my own fate.

And what people are saying about me is untrue. I am not a loose woman, a collaborator. How could a Jew be in with those Gestapo men?

Floriot: On the contrary, I would argue that this woman had every reason to help the Gestapo schemes – to save her own skin. A Jew, as she says, and from Romania. I put it to her that profited well from this arrangement. She lied then and is lying now. Why, she even took a German lover!

Kahan: He was not German. He was Austrian.

Floriot: So was a certain Adolf Hitler.
 Your landlady had German lovers. You were seen going to Gestapo headquarters in an army truck. You were seen in the company of German soldiers.

Kahan: My Austrian friend was with them. That's all. Things he told me I told on to the Resistance. Valuable things.

Mâitre Véron: There is no record of such information. No-one from the Resistance can confirm that. But there were bodies charred in 21, rue le Sueur who had been people you knew and who you never saw again once Dr Petiot had 'treated' them. Whose side were you really on?

Kahan: A woman in war has to be on one side. Her own.

Trials

Maître Véron: This 'doctor' was a false saviour and breaker of wild promises. His victims were flotsam of these dreadful times lured on to the rocks and their oblivion by this terrible man, this captain of death who was no pilot to the safe waters they had been promised. His so-called Resistance group was nothing but a ghostly vessel of promise. Imagine lost sheep finding their way to the shepherd only to be taken to the slaughter.

Petiot: Good God – what a mélange of mixed metaphors and desperate excuses for an argument!

Bells and whistles, false beards and pointed hats and wolf cries in the wings! What an opera this is.

Did you think that this was the show-piece of our times – you with your opera glasses crammed in to the back of this court. You gawpers and sighing molls....

If you want a trial of the true monsters of the war years then get on a train and travel to Nuremburg. They have spare seats there, I hear.

All this waste of good French time on a pack of lies and insinuations.

Maître Véron: And yet we shall all see you meet your fate. There is no escape for you. This farce shall end, believe me, Doctor Petiot in a tragedy for you.

Petiot: Go and pick at your scabs – I shall attend to my sketches of this grand farce. And my Fly-Tox comrades shall come out to avenge these wrongs! See – I sharpen my pencils.

Maître Véron: Ah, yes, the Fly-Tox fantasy. We have heard from those who have a better memory and a more honest spirit than that of the accused. That weight of evidence shall propel the blade of the guillotine: this madman, this monster, this perverted man of medicine shall meet justice and his fate.

Floriot's riposte

Your honour, gentlemen of the jury. I will not take the fifteen hours – fifteen hours, mind you – of the prosecution's desperate attempt to wear you down into an easy verdict. No, you have had enough to deal with, but there remain serious doubts and issues:

…and those suitcases, crucial pieces of evidence, it has been argued have been opened and re-sealed and opened again on so many occasions that the police and the prosecution cannot determine the number. Who has recorded accurately, who has removed or substituted items?

Then there is the question of the official court visit to 21, rue le Sueur on….

…and who could believe the evidence of this motley crew of criminals and collaborators?

…thought that they had seen Madame Khaït, but how serious was the police effort to verify this…

…the pipe, was it Petiot's?

… the hat claimed to be Braunberger's was not the correct size… the 'PB' initials could not have been those of the manufacturer's process…

…so, I put it to you, Jean Hotin's testimony is highly suspect…

…members of the Fly-Tox group would naturally have vanished back into society, to normal life…

…since admitting to the killing of those sent on by Eryane Kahan confirms my client's credentials as a patriot executing our enemies… the torture he suffered at the hands of the Gestapo…

…a war veteran who bore the scars of his sacrifice for France… re-born as an outstanding medical practitioner…

…pimps and whores, addicts and collaborators…

…the torture and horrors of rue Lauriston… the Milice… the Bonny-Lafont gang of thugs

…the witnesses warmly speaking to his municipal service in office in Villeneuve-sur-Yonne….

…patients treated without charge… cycling at night to save a young boy…

…the truth and lies and everything in between glimpsed through the darkness of an occupation…

…. And now in the calm after the storms of war, how many of our citizens are still missing, unaccounted for, lost to their families and France – for who knows how long? Forty thousand, fifty thousand? And might not some in that great lost generation be the supposed victims of this doctor? The people in extremis to whom he and his Resistance offered escape and freedom.

…Petiot stands before you, before France, as a patriot in the most painful of times, performing the most painful of necessary tasks.

Palais de Justice: Petiot

If I am guilty then God – wherever he is – will know, and no-one else.

What I have done was done for France – poor, violated France, who shall be strong again now that we have rid ourselves of the Boche rapist.

What we in the Resistance did was what all of France should have done and now should applaud.

What justice? What morality?

What is on trial here?

Germany is where you should be if you thirst for the justice of revenge – Nuremburg. The trains are still running, but be quick to see those monsters dealt with.

Look to Goering, Hess, Hans Frank – the murdering Nazis. Those pigs are drenched in blood – how many thousands – women, children – Belsen, Dachau. And those Russians too – I told our allies and so-called intelligence men about the Polish officers in the woods they slaughtered. Who was listening? And those I executed were vermin. I killed stooges, collaborators, bandits, Nazi arse-lickers. Fly-Tox saved the police and the Gestapo a job. Jo the Boxer and those tarts, the turncoat Jews, they'd have ended up on the trains from Drancy – to meat-hooks in the East. The dark forests where they say death has stopped the bird-song.

All this is ludicrous! Who didn't kill?

The Boches in France made everything a war. Not to kill the pigs and their whores and informers would have been the real crime. And I am no opportunist, Johnny Come Lately, who, seeing the way the war was going, the end-game in Paris, then picks up a gun and joins the fight when it is over. Petiot and Valéry never gave up the struggle. I bore arms for France in the First War and have done so again. My breast is proud – for a medal, not your swords!

And do not let those that collaborated think they have escaped us true Frenchmen. Do not let them rest in the shadows. The whole of France is heaving with revenge. I say hunt them down, as I did. Give them the bullet. Give them the rope. Cut the swastika into their tits, the tondues, the sheared whores!

Vive la France!

Cell 7: Magda visits

Do you remember me?
Which of us do your recall?
You treated me for a nervous condition
after my trial. Your counsel Floriot won my freedom,
but you are now surely beyond even his genius
for freeing the guilty.

How much did I tell you, eh?
That Magda Fontanges was Madeleine Coraboeuf
on the stage. An actress? I was more –
a journalist who met, interviewed and fucked Il Duce.
I should have been the one hanging from that lamppost
with him in a final dance through the air,
my legend secure.

But that bastard de Chambrun, our Ambassador,
had me thrown out of Italy
when I was making my way to the top.
I wanted revenge but only grazed him
with that shot on the platform
at Gard du Nord to greet his express from Rome.
Attempted murder – my arse!
My trial was the biggest, the hottest ticket in town,
before yours, of course.

I had soft dealings with several men of our government
as they waltzed through the shadows of the coming war.
Most of them deserved the prison you're in.
Who were you really playing for?
You and I played the long game and looked
after number one.

So what if I switched to the winners?
German agent 800G4 in Paris – was that me?
And was I the only woman to thrive, to survive?
My head is unbowed; I am not one of those
shaven and spat at along the boulevard.

Still, better to have survived, shamed, but alive,
which is more than you, doctor, will be
by the end of this week, our man Floriot's
firing blanks. And you falling asleep
in the dock as they read the litany of your crimes.
It goes badly for you, doesn't it?

You and I have been shaped by our times.
I remember Paul-Boncour,
the Foreign Minister of France,
his trousers around his ankles, crying
on my shoulder.
Later that evening he wrote to me:
To kiss your breasts I would ignore Czechoslovakia.

The Reporter, April 4th, 1946

The jury went out to consider their verdict just after nine that evening. My head was reeling after three weeks of this case and I'd had enough of the whole business. With over two dozen counts of murder I left them to it and went across to the Dauphin for my usual nightcap – two cognacs and a large black coffee – a full packet of Gauloises and three or four of the day's newspapers, our rivals – know your rivals.

Bugger me, I still had a third cognac and most of *Le Journal* left when there's this flurry of activity and men leaving their seats in a hurry. Rousseau spilled half his wine over my table and left his hat behind. The verdict!

Seems that they had taken barely two hours – two hours over that many cases, that many questions and issues. How many minutes had they spent on each capital offence? After weeks of arrogance and ill-advised humour from the accused, after the bewildering range of names and contacts and facts and counter-facts, a rogues gallery of witnesses, the jury were clearly in no mood for subtleties and prevarications. Petiot was always going to get what everyone was convinced he deserved. He'd done himself no favours.

The court was quickly jam-packed even at that late hour; I couldn't get much of a seat even in the press section. The verdict was greeted by a hullabaloo and enough flash-bulbs to light up half of Paris. As he was led down Petiot turned and called out, 'I must be avenged!' Though avenged for what, exactly, I could not say.

COPY TO EDITOR

The lawyer's hair gleams smooth and silk
under the court lights –
Mâitre Floriot, the eloquent voice of France.
He has no woman, never smokes,
but takes one glass of champagne
before each brilliant summing up.
It is said that Floriot could get Satan off the Eden rap
in a Paris court.

He answers Mâitre Dupin's fifteen hours –
"May Petiot soon go to join his victims,"
with six and a half hours of well-judged cunning,
bringing the court to its feet with applause –
a ringing in Petiot's ears, I think, he'll remember
as the Madame Guillotine kisses him,
that blade coming down the runners like a distant express
you'd run along the platform for, but miss.

Prison de la Santé, May 23rd 1946

At night this prison sounds like a small factory,
or a flop house at the end of a street one would not walk down.

At night these vultures hover above me
as if I could feed them.
They long to pick the bones of what they see
as my evil. Scraps of the truth.

A fart on their Bible!

Let them roost at rue le Sueur.

On this last journey I may lose
my head, but
I'll take all my luggage with me.

The Afternoon

Get me the News Desk.
Monsieur, the Petiot case,
your biggest story, I think, for some weeks.
I have something to sell.

No… it will cost you… listen.
Yes, sixty thousand francs… a photograph too….
another fifty for the negative… It is risky...
my position, monsieur, my reputation,
no trail must lead back to me.

You will have it, you know that:
your readers with such a photograph and account –
It will double your readership for a week.

Yes, it is a clear picture… the prison yard…
Madame Guillotine herself… my secret…

OK, a lens poking out from under my coat, Resistance fashion.

Yes, the head is quite clear, distinct. It is him.
the guillotine blade glints as it bites. Clean,
tasteful as things can be.

The face?
Why, what do you think?
The face is fixed in a smile.

Monsieur?
Monsieur?
Operator?

Cleaning up

That bastard certainly bled his fair share
at the end.
It's the arteries, you see,
severed and still the heart pumping it through.
Enough for four men –
Petiot, Eugène, Valéry and Wetterald.

This lot'll take some washing down and polishing
before we pack it up and send it on.
Which is why we drew lots for the job.
No-one joins up to work in a human abattoir,
and me and Jean and Emile, we got the short straw.

Sometimes they scream and have to be given
the medicine; not this one –
calm as a morning stroll down the fucking boulevard
for his morning coffee and croissant.

If you've got to go – and we've all got to go, haven't we –
then it could be worse than this:
Monsieur de Paris is a skilled operator,
he has sent hundreds on their way.

And Madame de Guillotine
has a wicked tongue,
but when she falls on you
it is quick and final. Goodnight.

A goodnight kiss.

That morning: May 24th, 1946

Juge d'instruction Goletty
turned faint at the thought of the guillotine.
Petiot, collar removed, neck shaved bare,

sat calmly writing
the final letters to his wife and son.
God knows what there was he could say to them.

But to the puking Goletty, it is recorded,
as he was walked to the courtyard:

"I am a doctor. Do you wish me
to give you an injection?"

4
Vive les Libres

Gérard Lablais

Mount Sinai Hospital, Toronto, May, 2000

My dear Maurice,

Some things maybe don't need saying. But we have to say them anyway.

Let me get things down.

You must know that you were always the centre of my life and my hopes for our family's future and this country rest assuredly with you and Rebecca and my grandsons. Sam and Aaron are a credit to you and the firm's business will be safe when they follow you into the office.

They say that a complicated operation is needed. I may not have long and that I may not leave this place. Do not cut short your European trip — these times away are so important if things are going to work out.

Well, I have had a long enough life and have seen many things. You know about your grandmother and I ending up in Canada after the war. Refugees, if they are fortunate, bring with them money and valuables. Rebecca now wears the ruby ring that was hers. Our wedding present to you. Grand-Mére Georgette also brought a helluva lot of spirit and the means to set up our new life.

You will not remember the early Quebec days and so you have been dyed in the wool Maple Leaf and Blue Jays guys your whole lives. This city has been good to us and the real estate money will see you and the kids safely through anything that is to come. The new century is yours and all that scare stuff about the world coming to an end this year and everything shutting down was so much bear shit, wasn't it?

Now that we know the airliners are still crossing overhead and the computers are not going down and the world will continue with its business, I wanted to share with you guys some of the things you should know.

Your Grand-Mère, may she rest in peace, was in your lives for the first ten years or so and you will remember how kind and generous she was before her final illness and her becoming unhinged and unfocussed. We all owe everything we have as a family to her strength and her determination. But that is not all.

You ask about our family in France. The Lablais were for generations honest workers of the soil and then in the factories and vineyards of the north-east. That photograph of Mamé Georgette and your grandfather has led you to ask questions. I should answer some of them. This is something that concerns us not at all when we are young and making our way, but can begin to concern us when we have families of our own.

Did you know, Maurice, that you were named after your uncle? He died in Auxerre years ago. And he was not Maurice Lablais, but Maurice Petiot. Which was our family name before we left France and came up to Canada.

Grand-Mère Georgette was a beauty, wasn't she? And such a positive person until the end. I only saw her really upset once in our time in Canada. Remember we took you back to Montreal in '67 for the World Expo? 'Man and His World'. We had rooms in the Manoir Sherbrooke. It was around the time of Georgette's birthday, her sixty-third. You wanted to see the space displays and go on the rides? She wanted to go and see Maurice Chevalier in the Autostade but your mother and I already had tickets for The Supremes, thinking she'd mind you for the evening. It kind of worked out in the end; she saw the old crooner. Your name-sake, maybe.

Let me remind you that was the year the Canadiens won the Stanley Cup and the Maple Leafs were nowhere — Go Les Habs!

Lablais Holdings did well out of the Île Notre Dame development and that's what set the firm on its later course. On that trip you had us ride the Mini-Rail through two whole circuits past all those national pavilions and were so excited to see the new model Alfa Romeo, a 'space car' you called it. And a couple of years later I bought an Alpha for your grandmother. A thing of beauty. Red. With piss poor electrics. As I warned her. But she loved that thing and kept it after she'd had to give up driving. That bad last year before she passed, I'd go over and start it up on her drive, so she could hear it. It wasn't a car for your mother, so we sold it on.

So, while your mother and I rode with you on that Mini-Rail, your Grand-Mére had taken a cab into the city where President de Gaulle of France made a speech that screwed up the whole celebrations. "Vive le Québec libre!"

On the news reel you can see the old French hawk gripping the microphone stands like the handlebars of a Tour de France rider. He's stood on the balcony of the City Hall like he owned it. Your Grand-Mére was in that cheering crowd, in her finery, the fur coat, the Chanel dress, her string of pearls, the pigeon's blood ruby ring, all for him. Later she told me that she had been in the crowds lining the Champs Élysées back in '44 when the General had liberated Paris. "J'ai pleuré les deux fois."

She was Georgette Petiot then. And you should know that she was there in Paris on her own. I was in school in the country, in Joigny, and your Grand-Pére was fighting in the Free French Forces of the Interior. Though under an assumed name. Many names and identities were switched about at that time. Noms de guerre, if you like.

That was before he became the most famous, or infamous, man in France. You will find a bunch of newspaper cuttings in a brown attaché in the old trunk in the basement. In the second drawer of my desk in the study you will find a copy of his book – an author. Le Hazard Vaincu. I have to tell you, it's a kinda crazy book with maybe some truths and some fantastical ramblings. I've never finished reading it. Dad was in jail and facing a death sentence, so he must have been a little bit fou. These are not easy things to remember and you should know them and then forget them. Move on, as we all must do.

We have never spoken about this. And now it is too late. I honestly do not remember much about him. He was not often at home and had medical business dealings we did not know about, all over the city. Our apartment at rue Caumartin was also his medical practice and he kept that private from us.

You will read, if you so wish, so much nonsense and such wild stories about what happened. All these years later, who knows? There have been some books and that awful de Chalonge film which is nothing more than a B movie.

Now we are Famille Lablais. We are Canadian, but proud of France too. Aaron and Sam will have lives that carry no part of what happened in the war in Paris. Keep this to yourself, or share with Rebecca and the kids in due course, as you see fit. The brown attaché. Those were unreal times in the occupied city. Some childhood I had. It was an age ago and another time and place like no other.

You guys are enjoying Europe. The Venice Canal and the Vatican. Buckingham Palace to come. And say a special hello to Paris for me. I will ask them to post this care of Le Meurice, where you will be staying by the weekend. Love you.

Things are getting dark for me here. It is going faster than I thought. Faster than the doctors thought. Another tube··· another injection···

Tomorrow, we'll see. Love to you guys···.

The people, the characters

11. Arno Breker (1900-91). Hitler's favourite sculptor. A retrospective exhibition at the Centre George Pompidou in Paris in 1981 was met with protests. In 1985 a dedicated museum was set up near Cologne.

21. Josef Goebbels taking time off from the war. In 1934 Adolph Hitler had been Mussolini's guest in Venice and had taken a Fascist march past in St Mark's Square. He visited the Biennale just two weeks before the Night of the Long Knives assassinations of his rivals. Breker's statues would fill the German Pavilion in the 1938 Biennale; it had been re-designed to reflect Nazi aesthetics.

23. This is the first of three excerpts from a German intelligence officer. They are fictions based on the memories of Ernst Jünger 1895-1998.

24. Ernst Jünger met Richard Hughes at a reception following the award of the Schiller Prize in 1974. Hughes signed and inscribed the book for him and it was last recorded at a Sotheby's auction in London in 2002. I met Richard Hughes at a conference in Harlech in 1976, the year he died. I have a signed copy of my paperback version.

39. In the suburb of Drancy much of the original modernist building by Beaudouin and Lods survives. The occupants now are largely immigrant people of colour. The French government took decades to acknowledge its role in the arrest and transportation of the Jewish population. At Drancy now there is a memorial, a railway wagon and a Shoah museum.

47, 116... Georgette Petiot (1904-?). She and their son Gérard (b.1928) could not be traced following the trial and execution of Marcel Petiot. Much of his remaining property and fortune must have enabled them to disappear and build new lives. See 176.

54. Simone de Beauvoir (1908-86). Most famous for Le Deuxième Sexe which when translated as The Second Sex in 1952 became a widely influential feminist book. She began to establish herself as a novelist and essayist during the war.

60. *Combat*: A newspaper of the Resistance set up in 1941 which survived in various forms until 1974. Writers included John-Paul Sartre and the editor in chief for four years was Albert Camus.

62. Picasso's life and work throughout the occupation may be seen as

problematic. It is debatable whether he could have done more to help his friend the poet and painter Max Jacob – see page 63.

62. Otto Richter survived the war and became a sales director for VW in Belgium.

63. Max Jacob (1876-1944). Poet, painter, critic. Even his conversion to the Catholic faith in 1909 could not save him. A Jew and probably a gay man; the Nazis arrested him at Saint-Benôit-sur-Loire.

72. Dietrich von Choltitz (1894-1966). A successful army commander who became the last military governor of Paris. He was released by the Allies in 1947. Among the listeners in the cellars at Trent Park were several European Jews who had escaped the Nazis, including the grandfather of the comedian Helen Lederer. The Trent Park recordings were to prove as valuable as the work at Bletchley Park. The eighteenth century house and estate had been owned by the Sassoon family, prominent Jewish bankers from Frankfurt; it is now a gated community where one-bedroom flats are on sale for £560,000.

78. General Charles de Gaulle (1890-1970). The dominant political figure of the three decades after the war; de Gaulle had an uneasy relationship with his former allies, though his rise to power after liberation effectively quashed the potential Communist rule of France. It may be possible to locate Georgette Lablais in photographs of the crowd beneath the balcony in Montreal in 1967.

80. Ernest Hemingway (1899-1961), one of the outstanding American novelists, he had seen action in the Great War, the Spanish Civil War and again after the Normandy landings. There is still a 'Bar Hemingway' in the Paris Ritz. He committed suicide by shooting himself.

83. 'Arletty' (Léonie Marie Julie Bathiat, 1898-1992). Her most famous film was 'Les Enfants du Paradis' made in the spring of 1945 in Nice, in Vichy France, with actors, crew and extras including Jews, Resistance fighters and Germans. She was prosecuted as a collaborator and imprisoned for a time in the Drancy Camp. In 1949 she played Blanche in the first French production of a *A Streetcar Named Desire*. She continued her affair with the officer Hans-Jürgen Soehring for several years after the war.

84. Lee Miller (1907-77) was a model for *Vogue* before becoming a war correspondent. She had lived with the photographer Man Ray in Paris before the war and moved in artistic circles. Her colleague David E. Shermann

took the iconic photo in Hitler's bath in Munich. In 1947 she married the English surrealist artist Roland Penrose. Her photographs can be seen at www.farleyshouseandgallery.co.uk

86. Maurice Chevalier (1888-1972). The singer was accused of collaboration and at one point was reported to have been assassinated by the Maquis. The probability was that he was blackmailed by the Nazis because he was helping Jewish friends in Vichy France. He sang in clubs and certainly went to perform for French prisoners in a POW camp in Germany, securing the release of ten prisoners. He had himself been incarcerated in the same camp in the First World War. Public workers, entertainers, hotel staff and others, could all have been accused of collaboration. Innocence and guilt under the Occupation and afterwards was problematic. By the time of the Montreal '67 World Expo, he had been completely re-established as an international singer and film star.

89. Dick Friedman later served in occupied Vienna and may have been one of the inspirations for the character of Holly Martins in Grahame Greene's The Third Man.

89. The 'goat woman' was Virginia Hall (1906-82) D.S.C. Hon. O.B.E. Croix de Guerre, parachuted into occupied France for the S.O.E. She nicknamed her wooden leg 'Cuthbert'.

90. Fred Astaire (1899-1987) is shown dancing in Place Vendôme in a brief clip on YouTube. He is moving towards the Vendôme Column which commemorates Napoleon's victory over the Russians; its bas-relief panels were made from cannons captured at the Battle of Austerlitz. Fred Astaire's birth name was Frederick Austerlitz.

91. Malcolm Muggeridge (1903-90), the writer and broadcaster who was a British intelligence officer in north Africa and then Paris observed: "Wherever de Gaulle appeared he was the government, and recognised as such." Which may go some way to explaining the 'Vive le Québec libre!' Quebec Libre debacle.

93. Coco Chanel (1883-1971). The leading fashion and perfume designer; liberator of women's fashion between the wars. Undoubtedly a collaborator, she had a Abwehr Agent number 7124, codename 'Westminster', but was not prosecuted, following to the intervention of Winston Churchill. When Marilyn Monroe said in 1952 that all she wore in bed was Chanel No5 she gifted the French designer the success that had eluded her when she had signed a contract to design for leading ladies in Hollywood with Sam

Goldwyn twenty years before. *The New Yorker* had pronounced that she had not grasped the need for film glitz: "She makes a lady look like a lady. Hollywood wants a lady to look like two ladies."

96. Samuel Beckett (1906-1989). It is clear that, like Simone de Beauvoir, his post-war writings have their roots in wartime Paris. Beckett was active in the Resistance, though a neutral Irishman; he returned to work as a volunteer to aid the restoration of St. Lô which had been heavily bombed by the Allies.

101. The D.G.E.R., the Direction Générale des etudes et des recherches was the wartime military security and intelligence service in wartime France.

103. René Floriot: Petiot's defence lawyer had already defended him in the Van Bever and Khaït cases concerning narcotics charges.

105. After the Liberation, Massu was accused of collaborating with the Germans. He was imprisoned, and in December of 1944 he attempted suicide by slitting his wrists. In the spring of 1945, a tribunal cleared him of all charges.

106. Pierre Bonny (1895-1944). A disgraced policeman who was credited with solving the Stavisky financial scandal in 1934, but was himself jailed on corruption charges the following year. The Bonny-Lafont gang were tolerated and then employed by the Germans and terrorized fellow Parisians.

113. Lt. Ayer as Captain Ayers was later implicated in the Bay of Pigs debacle. Agent Daughters was killed in a traffic accident in the French sector of occupied Berlin in 1948.

126. Petiot's time as doctor and then mayor of the picturesque town some 140 kilometres south-east of Paris was a period of rehabilitation after the traumas of the Great War. His achievements and crimes as a Communist politician are as confused and conflicted in memory and record as most other aspects of his life.

140. *Le Hasard Vaincu* or "Beating Chance" was a book of 360 pages with many doodles and illustrations which Petiot wrote during his months in prison and self-published in 1946. He used his three names in the text – Eugène, Petiot and Valéry: "This is a serious book that I am writing to amuse myself." He arranged for it to be privately printed. Remarkably, re-published in the last three years: one Amazon review praised its insights

into martingales. An original first printing copy is offered on AbeBooks with a dedication in Petiot's hand and a letter inserted: "During their interrogation, those whom you chose as medical experts questioned me about the assassination of the milkmaid of Villeneuve by stressing that the prescription prevented prosecution against me. If my lawyer had not confirmed it to me, I would not have believed that an allegedly serious case could contain a harvest of stupidities collected with care either from my political opponents who will stop at nothing to dirty me, or from Dangerous imbeciles who want to make themselves interesting by telling some novel in which they lend me words or facts (?)" The price – £4,500.

141. Pierre Véron represented both the Khaït families and the Dreyfus families. He had acted against Petiot in Madame Khaït's daughter's narcotics case.

154. Far-fetched as Petiot's claims may be, one should bear in mind the confusing nature of events at this time. "There are stories, lies and mis-remembering. We in the Résistance were necessarily wary of obvious truths." René Vallat, 'Le Renard Roux', interviewed in 1965.

191. The Nuremburg Trials of leading Nazis was in session at the same time as the Petiot case. It was rumoured that lawyers from Nuremburg were to visit the Petiot trial and that on one day a row of seats had been reserved for them.

197. Magda Fontages/Madeleine Coraboeuf (1905-60) was an actress, journalist and spy. Imprisoned in 1947 for collaboration and espionage.

204. 'Monsieur de Paris' – each of the city's executioners was thus named. The guillotine was first used in 1792 and last used in 1977. Its use was usually reserved for those condemned by civil law. Bonny and Lafont were shot.

208. Gérard Lablais Petiot's letter to his son Maurice appears here for the first time.

Acknowledgements

There are a number of books and articles about the Petiot case, or which refer to the events in occupied Paris. Many accounts are partial, several are contradictory in terms of timings and details. There are no reliable records of the court case and some serious questions about the nature of legal proceedings at this time. Paris was a city of chaos, confusion, recriminations and damage, physical, emotional and psychological. Some facts may be verified, many cannot. Some fictions are factions, some are not. History, metaphor and trope nudge against each other.

I first read about Dr Petiot in the early 1980s in John V. Grombach's *The Great Liquidator*. That is an age away and now there is a host of publications and web references readily available concerning the occupied city and Petiot, including film footage of the case. Some of these illuminate the matter, many serve only to complicate and confuse. As this book was going to press, there even appeared a comic book version of the case; it was not edifying. There are further details of all these reference points on my website – www.tonycurtispoet.com

We shall, probably, never know who Marcel André Henri Félix Petiot really was and what he really did, and why. I am an unreliable narrator to add to those who have already encountered this man, his times and the circumstances which led to his execution.

In the preparation and writing of this book I was able to share the text with a number of friends and members of my family: I wish to thank – Margaret and Gareth, Philip, Jenny, Hilary, Charlie, Geraldine, Chris, Colin, Ken, Amy and Peter; and Christine and Michael for their web research. And, of course, Mick Felton, my editor at Seren.

Photographs

7 – German occupation of Paris, World War II, June 1940.
Photo by Ann Ronan Pictures/Print Collector/Getty Images

25 – German soldiers on the terrace of a café in Paris.
Photographer unknown.

46 – The front page of *Le Matin*, 14 March 1944.
National Library of France.

74 – German officers relaxing in the grounds of Trent Park with their
British minders. Photographer unknown.

81 – Ernest Hemingway with American infantry.
Photo by Central Press/Getty Images.

94 – Winston Churchill and Charles de Gaulle, on the Champs Elysées.

99 – German prisoners in a Parisian street. Henri Cartier-Bresson.

104 – Marcel Petiot, shortly after his arrest. Photographer unknown.

115 – The front page of the *Daily Mirror*, 4 November 1944.

119 – Marcel and Georgette Petiot on the wedding day.
Photographer unknown.

128 – Doctor Marcel Petiot, 1921. Photographer unknown.

137 – Marcel Petiot, police record photograph.

142 – Petiot in the dock, during his trial. Photo by AFP via Getty Images)

145 – Petiot's Carte d'Identite for his Wetterwald alias.
Photographer unknown.

155 – The Petiot trial. Photo by Keystone-France\Gamma-Rapho via
Getty Images.

177 – Bastille Day During Nazi Occupation. Getty Images.

203 – Workmen prepare the guillotine before Petiot's execution.
Photographer unknown.

207 – Charles de Gaulle in Quebec, 1967. Photographer unknown.

A Note on the Author

Tony Curtis is an acclaimed poet who has published eleven collections. He has also published a volume of short stories and edited many anthologies and critical works. He has written extensively on war and on visual art, particularly in Wales. He led the Creative Writing department at the University of Glamorgan for many years. He is Emeritus Professor of Poetry at the University of South Wales and a Fellow of the Royal Society of Literature. Seren published his *From the Fortunate Isles: New & Selected Poems* in 2016. www.tonycurtispoet.com